MORE THAN
She Can Take

EROTICA SHORT STORIES, **VOL.28**

I0548341

JUST PLAIN BOB

WARNING

This book contains sexually explicit scenes and adult language. It may be considered offensive to some readers. This book is for sale to adults ONLY.

Please store your files wisely where they cannot be accessed by underage readers.

* * * * * * * * * * * * * * * * * * *

WANT FREE COPIES OF MY BOOKS?
Just visit my blog and download free copies of my books:
awesomeauthors.org/justplainbob

About the Publisher

4Fun Publishing, a member of **BLVNP Incorporated**, 340 S. Lemon #6200, Walnut CA 91789, info@blvnp.com / legal@blvnp.com
NOTE: Due to the highly emotional reaction of some people to works of erotic fiction, any email sent to the above address that contains foul language or religious references is automatically deleted by our anti-spam software and will not be seen. All other communications are welcome.

DISCLAIMER

Please don't be stupid and kill yourself. This book is a work of FICTION. Do not try any new sexual practice that you find in this book. It is fiction and not to be confused with reality. Neither the author nor the publisher or its associates assume any responsibility for any loss, injury, death or legal consequences resulting from acting on the contents in this book. Every character in this book is over 18 years of age. The author's opinions are not to be construed as the opinions of the publisher. The material in this book is for entertainment purposes ONLY. Enjoy.

Erotica Short Stories, Vol. 28

More Than She Can Take

10 Sexy Stories in 1

By: Just Plain Bob

ISBN: 978-1-68030-426-8

Table of Contents

Tiffany

I flirt with the ladies. It is just something that I did. I did it without even thinking about it; it just comes out naturally. None of them were ever going to take me up on anything I said and I knew it. Christ, I was fifty-two years old and the girls I flirted with were all in their twenties and were married or had boyfriends. Besides, they all knew my wife and thought that we were happily married.

We weren't. Weren't happily married I mean, and hadn't been since the day, two years ago, when I found her in bed with another man. Harry Wiggins had cut his hand on the job and the boss had me drive him to the emergency room at the hospital. It was close to lunchtime so while Harry waited for them to do whatever it was that they were going to do, I thought I'd run home for lunch.

That was something that I had never done before because I only got half an hour for lunch break and the house was twenty minutes from work. There was a car that I didn't recognize in the driveway and I figured that Lois had some girlfriend over. I knew that wasn't so as soon as the front door closed behind me.

The loud, "Fuck me, fuck me, fuck me," coming from the bedroom upstairs told me what was going on. I walked up the stairs and down the hall to a chorus of "Oh yes, oh yes, harder baby, harder, don't stop, I'm almost there, don't stop now."

The bedroom door was open and I stood in the doorway and watched some man I'd never seen before fuck Lois from behind while she cried, "Oh yes baby, fuck me, fuck me hard. Jesus, I can never get enough of your cock baby, I love your cock. Give it to me baby, give it to me."

Her head was on a pillow and she was on her knees and from where I stood in the doorway, I couldn't tell whether he was in her ass or pussy, but then it didn't really matter – it was still infidelity. They hadn't noticed me and I stood there debating on whether to wade in swinging or just yell out, "Honey, I'm home" and watch them scramble, but in the end, I did nothing. I turned and left the house and went back to the hospital to wait for Harry.

<<O>>

I never did tell Lois that she had been busted. I just accepted the fact that she was an unfaithful whore and let it go. I had no idea how long it had been going on and no idea why. I had thought that we had a good marriage and I know, or at least I thought I did, that there was nothing wrong with our sex life. We made love three and sometimes four times a week, sometimes twice in a night and I was willing to do anything that she wanted. What was important, however, is that the marriage was dead – not over, just dead.

Why not over? Because I didn't have the energy for it. I'd been married once before and my first divorce had ruined me financially and had made me into an emotional basket case for years. If I was thirty-five or forty, I might have done it, but not at fifty. Why start over? Lois kept a clean house, was a good cook, and did the laundry and all the other things that a wife does to make life move smoothly. We didn't argue or fight so I just decided to settle for a comfortable existence. So I said nothing about what I saw and life went on.

The only change was that I stopped having sex with Lois. When she asked why, I told her that I was having some problems and was seeing a doctor. After two months, I told her that I had acute erectile dysfunction and that I couldn't get a hard on. Another two months went by and then I told her that I had tried everything that the doctor had suggested, but that nothing worked and she would just have to get used to the fact that the sexual part of our marriage was over. She wasn't really happy about it, but I really didn't give a shit about how she felt about it.

I didn't give up sex though. There was a woman I went to high school with and she had lost her husband in the First Gulf War and she supplemented her income by servicing a few select customers and I paid her a visit twice a week.

Lois and I were in the habit of going out for breakfast every Saturday and Sunday and we always ate at the same restaurant. The place was just around the corner from where I worked and I had lunch in there two or three times during the week. There was a waitress working there named Tiffany and she was a lot of fun to be around. A tall girl, almost six feet, and with a hard, tight body to die for. She had the goods and she knew how to dress to show them off. Low hip-huggers and tops that emphasized her high breasts and flat stomach. She had a wild side to her and she had several tattoos and a piercing or two that she also loved to show off.

I got in the habit of flirting with her at lunchtime and after a couple of months, we had developed a rapport. The flirting progressed from the simple to the borderline raunchy and Tiff gave as good as she got. She had a stud through her tongue and one day I said, "One of these days you are going to have to explain or better yet, show me what the purpose of that thing is."

She stuck her tongue out at me and said, "First you will have to show me that your health insurance is up to date. When I put you in the hospital I want to know that you'll be taken care of."

One day when I came in after not stopping in for a week, she came up to my table and lifted her top to show me that she'd had her navel pierced and was sporting what looked like a diamond stick pin.

"You know, Tiff, I have a barely controllable urge to kiss your belly."

"I'd let you, but then you'd want to see the one farther down and if I let you see that one I'm afraid you would have a heart attack. I can't afford to lose any of my good tippers."

This kind of banter went on for months and then one day, I came in to find that Tiff wasn't her usual cheery self.

"Got a problem, Tiff?"

She slid into the booth across from me. "My asshole boyfriend just told me to move out. He said he was moving to Durango and was going to sell the house. Then he told me that when he got set up there, he'd let me know and that I could join him. No talking about it at all. Just get out and I'll give you a call when I'm ready for you again."

"You going to be all right?"

"Yeah, I guess. I can stay with my girl friend for a while until I can find a place."

Then she got up and went back to work.

<<O>>

From then on, every time I'd see her, I'd ask how it was going and I'd get an update. One Saturday, while at breakfast with Lois, I asked how she was doing and she said, "Okay, but me and my girl friend aren't getting along all that well and I'm looking for another place to stay."

"I'd offer you the use of our spare bedroom, but I don't think Lois here would be too happy about it. It would piss her off to know I'd be chasing you around the house every chance I got."

I know what Lois was thinking when I said that. "Yeah, and when you caught her, you could sit down and play checkers or something."

Lois might have been an unfaithful whore, but she did have a lot of good qualities and she found Tiffany a place to stay, at least for a little while. She had a friend who was going abroad for a month and who was looking for a reliable house sitter for while she was gone. Lois got Tiffany the deal. In retrospect, I guess you could say that what finally happened, Lois brought onto herself because I doubt that it would have happened had Tiff not gotten the house-sitting gig.

<<O>>

Once Tiff started house-sitting, things began to happen. Her car started having problems and I offered to stop by after work and take a look at it. It had a hundred things wrong with it and every night I would stop by and do a little work on it. Tiff would ask me in for coffee when I was done for the evening, and since she was rather casual in the way she dressed around the house, I had ample opportunity to see her flat stomach, the long supple legs, and a hint of tit every once in a while. In short, she pretty much kept my dick hard.

In addition to her various piercings, Tiffany also had several tattoos, two of which I could never see all of. One was down so low on her belly that I could only see the top third of it when she wore very low cut hip-huggers. The other was on the inside of her left tit and I could only see about an inch of it sticking up above her bra or bikini top. I started joking with her about what I would have to do to see the entire tattoo. She would laugh and say, "Only my lover gets to see all."

Then the month was over, Lois' friend came back, I had Tiffany's car running and it was back to just seeing her at the restaurant.

We kidded and flirted like crazy and some of the other regulars began to think that we had something going. One day, one of them asked me how an old fart like me was managing to keep up with a young fox like Tiffany. It was only then that I realized that I wished I actually could.

Two days later, Tiff slid into the booth across from me and told me that she had given two-week's notice.

"Dave called last night and said he was ready for me."

"Are you sure that you really want to do this? He screwed you over once; do you really want to move yourself three hundred miles so he can do it again? At least when he did it here, you had some people you could fall back on."

She didn't say anything, just got up and went back to work. I saw her three more times before she was due to leave, but the kidding around and flirting were gone. I didn't realize what a hole her going was going to leave in me. On what was supposed to be her last day, I stopped by to say goodbye, but she wasn't there. I'd brought a card wishing her good luck and I left it with one of the other waitresses in case she came in. It was still sitting next to the cash register two days later. I asked Becky if Tiff had not come in and she told me that Tiff would be back to work the following Monday.

"What happened?"

"You'll have to ask her."

I changed my schedule the following Monday. I left the house two hours earlier so I could stop and have breakfast on my way to work. Tiff was there and when she came to take my order she handed me back my card.

"Thanks, it was sweet of you, but I can't use it."

"What happened?"

"I listened to you. When I got to Durango, the first thing Dave said to me was, "It's about damned time you got here." His attitude sucked and then I remembered what you said about how he had screwed over me once and how could I be sure that he wouldn't do it again. It took me three minutes to tell him I'd only made the trip so I could tell him goodbye in person and now here I am."

"What are you going to do now?"

"I'm staying with my Uncle Ralph until I can find a place."

"If I can help, let me know."

She reached down and touched my cheek with her hand and said, "You're sweet, Mike. Thank you, I'll keep it in mind."

It was two days before I saw her again and asked her how her search for a place was going.

"Not good, but I need to find something quick."

"Things not going well at your uncle's?"

"I'm not comfortable there. I don't know why, but I feel that I have to lock the bedroom door when I'm there."

<<O>>

That night when I got off work, I went to see a friend of mine who managed some apartments. I found out that he had a couple of vacancies and I told him that I wanted one of them. I had to work hard to convince him that I wasn't setting up a little love nest and I don't think I managed to do it because all he said was, "Okay, Mike, whatever you say."

"I'm serious, Dave. She's just a good kid that I've taken a liking to and I'm just trying to help her out. She can afford the rent, but there isn't any way that she could put down the last month's rent and security deposit. I'll put those up. When I send her over here, just rent her the place and don't tell her about that, okay?"

"Sure, Mike, whatever you say," he said with a grin that fairly screamed out, "You old stud."

"I'm serious, Dave. Don't tell her what I've done, that will only complicate things."

Same grin, "Sure, Mike, whatever you say. My lips are sealed."

<<O>>

The next morning, I left for work early and I stopped by the restaurant for breakfast. When Tiffany waited on me, I told her that I had found her an apartment and I gave her the address and told her to ask for Dave. The next day, Tiffany caught me coming in the door and she threw her arms around me and gave me a big hug.

"Thank you, Mike. Thank you, thank you, thank you," and then she kissed me on the cheek. I was just a little embarrassed by it especially since the place was full of customers, but what really bothered me was the rock-hard erection I got when she pressed her soft body into mine. I just hoped that she hadn't felt it.

The next day was Saturday and when Tiff came to wait on Lois and me, I asked her if she'd found a new boyfriend yet.

"Not yet. There aren't that many guys out there willing to date a girl as tall as I am. I think it makes them feel insecure when they have to look up at me or when I look down at them."

Lois said, "You know, Mike, I think Robbie would be perfect for her."

"Who is Robbie?" Tiff asked.

"Robbie is our son," Lois said. Actually, he was my son from my first marriage, but he had been calling Lois mom since the day I married her.

"How old is he?"

"He's thirty-one, dear, and he is six feet four so I don't think your height is going to bother him."

"He sounds perfect, but what's the catch?"

"Catch?"

"Yeah. Thirty-one and not married?"

"I don't know, dear. He just tells us that he hasn't found the right one yet."

Monday at lunch, Tiff slid into the booth across from me.

"Mike, can I get personal for a second?"

I shrugged and said for her to go ahead.

"You worked on my car and didn't ask for anything. You found me an apartment and now you are trying to fix me up with your son? What gives?"

I jokingly said, "What the hell, Tiff, if I can't have you, at least I can try to keep you in the family."

Her face changed and I couldn't read her expression. She reached over and touched my hand and in a low voice she said, "But you can have me, Mike. I thought that you knew that," and she got up and left me sitting there stunned. I had never expected anything like that to happen. All I had done was be nice to a girl that I had taken a liking to. Sure, I had flirted with her and yes, it had gotten a little raunchy at times with some sexual overtones, but that was just a dirty old man having some fun and we all knew that, right?

I was numb when I went back to work. Numb, confused, and not just a little bit excited. I remembered how she had felt when she had hugged me and the erection I had gotten from holding her close. I remembered the thoughts I'd had when I saw her pierced navel and I remembered how I had reacted the day Fred asked me how an old fart like me was managing to keep a girl like Tiff happy.

For all of twenty seconds, I thought about how wonderful it would be to be with Tiffany and then reality set in. Age alone was enough to drive a stake through that thought. She was a baby for Christ's sake. She was eight years younger than my son – the son that Lois wanted to set Tiffany up with. It was impossible, it could never happen, but the thoughts had me so horny that I almost – only almost – went after Lois for sexual satisfaction.

<<O>>

The next two days at lunch, I was a little on the subdued side. No flirting, no how-are-you-doing questions, just smiled and gave my order. On the third day, Tiff slid into the booth across from me and handed me a piece of paper.

"What is it?"

"Open it and read it."

I opened it and saw that it was blank except for the number 201 written in the middle of the paper.

"That is what you can consider as an engraved invitation to get your ass over to our apartment."

"Our apartment?"

"Mike, I'm young, but I am not a dumb bimbo. I know two other people who live in that apartment complex and I know all about first and last months' rent and security deposits and since I didn't have to put them up that means that you did. That makes it our apartment. It is seven minutes from your parking place at work to a parking place at the apartments. You get off at four-thirty and if you are not at the door to our apartment by four forty-five, don't bother to come in here to eat anymore because if you do I'll make your life miserable – up to and including spitting in your food."

She got up and left. When she came back with my order, she smiled and set it down in front of me and said, "Four forty-five" and then she went and waited on other customers.

Believe it or not, I wrestled with the idea all afternoon. I wanted to go, but I knew that no good could come of it. In the end, I decided that I should go, thank Tiff for thinking so highly of me and then explain why I needed to be heading on home. Surely I could make her understand that the almost thirty-year age difference would doom us right from the start. I would do "The Right Thing" and then find some place else to have breakfast and lunch.

My resolve to do the right thing disappeared when Tiff answered my knock. She was wearing a cut off T-shirt that let me see the lower half of her breasts and the tightest pair of cut off Levi's shorts that I had ever seen. She stepped aside and let me in and as she closed the door behind me I turned to her and opened my mouth to speak, but she put a finger up to my lips.

"Shush up, Mike. I know what you are going to say and I have no intention of listening to it. I don't care about the age difference and I don't care that you are married. I want you and I'm pretty sure that you want me. That's all we need for right now. You don't have to say a word and in fact, I would just as soon you didn't. You once told me that you wanted to kiss my belly and I think that would be a great place for you to start. Where you go from there is up to you."

It was an evening that most men can only dream about. If it could be done between a man and a woman, Tiffany and I did it. Some of her youth must have been transferred into me because she was able to take me longer and farther than I had gone in years. When I reached the point where I knew that I just couldn't go on, Tiff would give me a wicked little smile, work some magic and we would be off running again.

But finally even Tiffany's magic wouldn't work anymore. She was still trying, but to no avail. While trying, she asked me what time I had to be home.

"When I get there."

"Won't Lois wonder if you stay out late?"

"She probably will, but I'm not going to worry about it."

"I'm not trying to break up your marriage, Mike."

"You can't hurt it, Tiff. It doesn't exist except maybe in Lois' mind."

"I don't understand?"

So I explained to Tiffany what had happened and how I had decided to handle it."

"I'd never have believed that looking at the two of you. She loves you, that much is obvious. I can tell from the way that she looks at you."

"I don't know. Maybe she does in her own way, but my definition of love doesn't include a strange man in my bed."

"Well, she does love you. Women can tell about things like that. Why she did what she did I don't know, but trust me on this, Mike, she does love you."

"It really doesn't matter to me any more, Tiff. Right now the only thing that is important is that you know that nothing that you and I do can hurt my marriage. But that does bring us to just what it is that you expected out of this."

"As much as I can get, lover, and for as long as I can get it. I'm not stupid. I know that the age difference is a killer. We won't like the same music, read the same books or like the same TV shows. All my friends will think I'm crazy for wasting my time with an old geek like you and all of your friends will laugh at you for trying to go back and regain your youth by banging a young bimbo. We just have to take what we can get when we can get it. If we can make it last for years and years, good for us. If we can't, well, at least we had a good time and no regrets. Will that work for you?"

"Since it is the best offer on the table, I guess I'll just have to take it, won't I?"

"There is one more thing, baby, will it bother you that I'm married?"

The confusion on my face must have been evident because she went on, "Dave is really my husband. I don't wear my rings and I called him my boyfriend because I got better tips as long as the guys thought that they might have a chance. I'm not going back to him, but I'm not going to waste money on a divorce lawyer either. If there is a divorce, Dave can pay for it."

I had to smile at that. "Well, Tiffany, if you can put up with my being married, I guess that I can accept the fact that you are."

I had learned some harsh lessons from my first divorce and while I had no intention of wasting money on lawyers to get a divorce from Lois, I had no idea of what she might do when I move out and went to live with Tiffany. For the next two weeks, I spent my evenings after work with Tiff and then went home to Lois, but during the day, I quietly closed out CDs and withdrew money from savings. My 401k at work had a provision that allowed me to borrow against it up to fifty percent and so I did. When I felt that I had protected myself financially as best I could, I went home and dropped the bomb on Lois.

"You are what?"

"I'm moving out."

"That's it? You just walk in the door and tell me that you are moving out?"

"That pretty much sums it up."

"After all these years and I don't even get an explanation?"

"I've found someone else, Lois, someone I'd rather be with than you."

"You would rather be with than me? For God's sake, Mike, why? How can you take our marriage and just toss it away? I thought you loved me?"

"At one time I did, Lois. At one time you were my life, but then you stopped loving me and that killed something inside me and now I'm moving on."

"What are you saying? I've never stopped loving you, Mike. I love you as much now, if not more, as I did the day I married you."

"Then you must not have loved me all that much on that day, Lois, or you would never have done what you did to me."

"Mike, you're being stupid. I don't know what it is that you think I've done to you, but I've never stopped loving you. I don't care who it is that you think is so special, but she can never love you the way I do."

"She already has Lois."

"Come on, Mike, think it through. You think that you have something with this woman, but how long can it last when she finds out that you can't perform sexually. It doesn't matter to me because I love you for who you are, not for what you can do."

"I perform for her quite well, Lois, sometimes as many as three or four times a night."

"I don't understand. You haven't been able to make love to me in over two years."

"I've been able, Lois, I just didn't want to."

"What are you saying, Mike? You love me, I know you do."

"No I don't, Lois. I did. I did, right up to the day I came home from work at lunchtime and found you in our bed with another man. Your cries of, 'Oh baby I can never get enough of your cock, give it to me, give it to me' drove a stake through the love I had for you. There was never anything wrong with my dick, Lois, I just didn't want to touch you after that."

Lois turned pale when I said that. "You weren't supposed to know, you weren't ever supposed to know," she said in a low, weak voice. "It didn't mean a thing, Mike. He means nothing to me. It was just sex, baby, that's all it was. I just needed more than I was getting, baby. Honest to God, Mike, he means nothing to me. I love you, honey, only you."

"Well, look on the bright side, Lois. I'm out of here so you can move him in and fuck for twenty-four hours a day. That way you can get as much as you need."

The last thing I heard as I walked out the door was, "Don't do this to me, Mike, I love you.   Don't leave me, Mike, honest to God, I love you."

I guess that maybe she did. She never filed for divorce and I get calls from her at work every week. She sent me a card on my birthday and signed it, "Waiting, love, Lois." I got one from her on Valentine's Day that was signed, "Yours forever. I love you and I'll wait for you for as long as it takes."

It didn't take long for her to find out about Tiffany and she stops at the restaurant every Saturday and Sunday and tells Tiff that she intends to get me back. If it is a slow day, Tiff will sit down with her and they talk. Lois says she is going to get me back and Tiff tells her that she should never have let me get away and Lois says, "Hey, I made a big mistake, but I still love him."

Despite the age difference, Tiff and I seem to be making it work, but the relationship is still in its infancy so only time will tell, but for the moment I'm living every dirty old man's dream. I have a young, beautiful, and sexy nympho on my hands and I'm holding on for dear life.

End of the 1st Story

Did She

She ground her pussy down on my face as she harshly said, "That's it, asshole, suck him out of me. Lick every drop of his cum out of me and you had best not miss one speck of it if you ever want me to fuck you again. You do want to fuck me again, don't you? Of course you do, so eat my pussy, baby, clean me out."

Twenty minutes later, she came out of the shower to find me sitting on the edge of the bed waiting for her. "Why? Why did you do it, why did you do that to me? Didn't you even care about what it would do to our marriage?"

"To answer your questions in order, sweetie; one, I did it because you called me a bimbo and that is what bimbos do. Two, I did it to you because I could, and three, I knew that it wouldn't do anything to our marriage. You love me and you won't do a fucking thing that might piss me off and make me leave. And four, even though you haven't asked, yes I do plan on doing it again – lots – and you will suck my lover's juices out of me each and every time if you want to keep me as your wife. Now, I have washed my lover's smell off me, do you want to fuck me or not?"

<<O>>

Well, she was right about a couple of things, but I wasn't so sure about some others. I had called her a stupid bimbo, I did love her and one time I had told her that I loved her so much that there wasn't anything that she could do that would drive me away, but then what she had just done wasn't something that I ever imagined that she would do. Calling Chrissi a stupid bimbo wasn't exactly a good move on my part and I should have known better. Chrissi was a fiery red-head with a temper to match and I knew that she would react to what I'd called her, but I had never considered that she would do something so overwhelmingly stupid to get back at me.

The whole thing had started because I very stupidly did not shit-can the invitation that came informing us of the time and date of Chrissi's ten-year class reunion. I had been smart enough to pitch mine the previous year and only God knows why I left hers out where she could find it. Once she had it in her hand, there was nothing that was going to stop her from going and I really, really didn't want to do that.

<<O>>

Chrissi had been one year behind me in high school and while I knew who she was, I didn't know her. I would have loved to know her, but we didn't travel in the same circles and an opportunity to meet her never arose. I watched her move from boy to boy like a butterfly flitting from flower to flower and several times I overheard locker-room conversations about what great head she gave and about how hot her pussy was. I heard rumors of how hot she was and how much fun you could have with her on the back seat of your car, but I had no way of knowing whether it was the truth or just wishful thinking on the part of the guys. Three months before I graduated, she started going steady with John Markham. Six weeks later, I heard him bragging about how he had popped her cherry (which indicated that the rumors were false or that John was a liar) and a week after that they got into a fight and broke up. Chrissi went back to being a butterfly and the rumors started up again. I graduated and headed off to college.

The beginning of my second year, I was in the campus bookstore buying books when I saw Chrissi and John walking down the aisle holding hands. We passed each other and there were nods of recognition and we moved on. After that, I saw her everywhere, sometimes with John and sometimes alone and she always waved or nodded when she saw me. One night I was in Augustinos, a pizza place just off campus, when she and John came in. They had been there for maybe twenty minutes when they got into a loud argument and John got up and stormed out of the place leaving Chrissi sitting alone at the table. She kept watching the door, but when he hadn't returned after ten minutes, she started looking around the place and saw me. For the next five minutes or so, she kept glancing over at me and finally she got up and walked over to the booth where I was sitting.

"Hi."

"Good evening."

"Can I sit down with you?"

"Be my guest."

She sat down and said, "We've never met" and she stuck out her hand, "I'm Chrissi" and I took her hand and shook it and said, "I know, I'm Tim."

She silently eyed me for a moment or two and then she said, "Look, this is awkward as hell for me, but I have a problem and you are the only face in here that I recognize. My date just walked out on me leaving me stuck with the tab and no way home. I have enough money on me to either pay the tab or take a cab home, but not enough to do both."

I smiled at her, "I've always wanted to be the knight in shining armor riding to the rescue of the fair damsel. How would you like to be saved? I can pay the tab so you can call a cab or you can pay the tab and I'll give you a ride home."

"You would do that for me? You're sweet. How about I pay the tab and you give me a ride home. That way I can thank my knight in shining armor properly."

The ride to her place was full of conversation about high school, who we had as mutual friends and other things like that. I walked her to her door and she turned to face me, "Thank you for rescuing me" and then she leaned forward and kissed me and I felt it all the way down to my toes. She stepped back, handed me a piece of paper and said, "Call me" and then she turned and went inside.

This took place during midterms and I was super busy cramming for exams and pulling all-nighters and I never did get around to calling Chrissi. A week went by and then one day, as I was having lunch in the Student Union, Chrissi came in, saw me, and came over and sat down. I said hi and she just looked at me for a second.

"I'm not used to kissing a guy goodnight, asking him to call and then not having him do it."

"I make no excuses, my lady. I had reasons, but I offer no excuses."

"Reasons? What kind of reasons?"

"I was in the middle of midterms and got caught up cramming and pulling all-nighters. Also, you and John are a couple and I never mess around with another man's woman."

"Okay, I'll buy the need to study, but if you look real close at my fingers you won't see any rings. I am not and I never will be another man's woman until I walk down the aisle and say "I do." Also, regarding John, that asshole is history. You have my number" and she got up and left.

I called Chrissi the next day, we dated, started going steady, got engaged and were married three months after graduation. Our six-year marriage had been a good one although there were a few rough spots that only I knew about and I managed to work through them without letting Chrissi know. They were mostly things caused by the fact that I am basically insecure. Even though I am married to Chrissi, I had never been able to convince myself that I deserved her. I always had the thought in the back of my head that she took me because she couldn't get what she really wanted.

Chrissi was a fun loving girl and she attracted attention wherever we went. At parties, she was always being asked to dance by other guys and she would badger me until I gave in and said yes. I've seen her get felt up on the dance floor, I've watched men slip her pieces of paper with their phone numbers on them and I saw her suck up the attention like a sponge. I never saw her push away a hand that slipped down to her ass or that found its way to one of her breasts and I never saw her fight off an attempt to get her in a dark corner where some kisses and some grab-ass could take place. When it happened, it ate at me like an ulcer.

But I never called her on her behavior because she always told me about it. On the ride home from wherever it was where we had been she would say, "Guess what Tom tried to do tonight" or maybe, "Harry is a pretty good kisser. He got me in a corner tonight and worked me over pretty good. I might even have a bruise on my left boob. He got me hotter than hell, baby, you need to hurry up and get us home. Speed if you have to, lover, I need it bad. Get me home and fuck me." I don't think that she ever ran around on me behind my back, but I don't know for sure that she didn't. Many were the times when I thought she just might have.

So there we were, Mr. Insecurity and Mrs. Good Time Girl, going back to her old stomping grounds. Going back to where she would be with all of her classmates and in particular, those classmates who, whether true or not, had talked about all the marvelous blow jobs and back-seat sex that they had had with Chrissi. I could have come up with an excuse that would have kept me home, but Chrissi still would have gone. I had to weigh it in my mind – would it be better to go and be a presence, a wet blanket as it were, or stay home and let my imagination drive me crazy? In the end, I realized that I had to go, but the bottom line was that I did not want to go, I really, really did not want to go.

It was every bit as bad as I had feared. All of Chrissi's ex-boyfriends flocked to her like bees to honey and every one of them wanted to dance with her. I got maybe one dance out of five and was able to break things up a bit, but Chrissi was still Chrissi and her behavior on the dance floor at the reunion was even more outrageous than it had been at home.

During one of our dances, Chrissi said, "I hope you have been taking your vitamins, lover, because I'm going to destroy you when we get to bed tonight. I'm horny as a goat right now and the night's just getting started. The only thing that hasn't happened out there on the dance floor is that I haven't been finger-fucked."

And then it got worse, at least for me. Two hours into the evening, John showed up at the affair. I saw him come in the door and he stopped and looked around the room for a minute and then he spotted Chrissi on the dance floor. He walked out onto the floor and tapped Chrissi's partner on the shoulder and cut in. They finished the dance and then Chrissi led him back to our table.

"Look who I found. I asked him to join us."

From that point on, except for the occasional dance with me, John was the only one that Chrissi danced with. When they danced, John had his hands all over her and Chrissi didn't protest even once. I had gotten up and gone to use the bathroom and when I came back into the ballroom, I didn't see Chrissi at our table or out on the dance floor. I scanned the room and spotted her over in a dark corner with John. They were exchanging a long, slow, lingering kiss and John had his hand down the front of Chrissi's skirt. She was standing just a bit spread-legged and I knew without seeing that he had his fingers either on or in her pussy. I was torn. Should I break things up and create a scene that would imprint this reunion on minds of everyone there or go sit at our table and sulk? I finally decided that ruining the reunion for everyone else was not something that I should do so I went and sat down at our table.

Several minutes later, Chrissi and John came back to the table and John excused himself to go to the bathroom. Chrissi took a sip of her drink and looked at me.

"What's the matter sweetie? You look upset."

"Me? Upset? Why should I be upset? Just because I see my wife in a dark corner kissing a guy while he finger fucks her? No, that couldn't be it, could it? Maybe it is something else. Like maybe the way everyone in this place is looking at me with pity in their eyes while my wife acts like a stupid bimbo with all her ex-boyfriends."

Chrissi had been in the process of raising her drink to take a sip when I said that and the glass came down and slammed on the table.

"So I'm a bimbo, am I? A stupid bimbo?"

Just then John came back and Chrissi stood up and took his arm, "Come on, John. We need to find a dark corner and get back to what we were doing," and she led him off. I watched them go and then I finished my drink, got up, and went back to our hotel.

I hit the hotel bar and sat there drinking until last call and then I went up to our room. Chrissi wasn't there, but then I hadn't really expected her to be. I put myself to bed and tried to fall asleep, but the image of Chrissi standing there with her legs slightly spread while John had his hand down her skirt just would not go away. I tossed and turned for a good hour before falling into a fitful sleep.

I didn't hear her come in. The first I knew that she was there was when she settled on top of me. I came awake to see Chrissi straddling my chest and looking down at me.

"Wakey wakey, hubby dear. Your stupid bimbo is home and she is bearing gifts for you."

She slid forward until her pussy was just above my mouth and she said, "Look at all the good, creamy white stuff I brought you. Its protein baby and protein is good for you," and she jammed her cunt down on my face. Her legs had my arms pinned to the bed and I thrashed and bucked, but I couldn't shake her off. Her cunt was covering my nose and mouthed and I opened my mouth to try and get some air and goop ran out of her cunt and into my mouth. I had to swallow or choke and ask I gulped the first batch down another glob ran in. Chrissi shifted position and that freed up my nose to breathe as she ground her pussy down on my face and harshly said, "That's it, asshole, suck him out of me."

I looked at her like she was an escapee from a mental institution and said, "What?"

"I said that I've washed his smell off me and I asked if you wanted to fuck me or not."

"You can't be serious. You can't do what you have done and expect me to do anything but end our relationship. Just leave me alone, Chrissi, just stay the fuck away from me. I'll try to be civil to you until we get home and I can find me an apartment, but until then, just stay away from me."

Chrissi's face turned pale and then she said, "You really think that I would do that to you?"

"Obviously you did do that to me."

"No I did not! I could never do that to you and you should know it."

"Well I don't know it, Chrissi, and what's more, I have never known it. I had always hoped that it was just touchy feely fun and that you never called any of those phone numbers or took calls from the men who gave them to you, but I never knew for sure. But tonight tore it, Chrissi. I saw you standing there with your legs spread and letting John finger-fuck you and that tore it. That and the absolute contempt that you showed that you had for me when you got up and went back to what you were doing. Every eye in that place was on me when I got up and left and all I saw was pity and looks that called me a wimp for putting up with your behavior."

"I always told you about what happened, I never hid anything from you and I would have told you about tonight. Yes, I did let John get away with a few liberties tonight and I did it on purpose. I led him on so he would think he was going to get some. I hold grudges, baby, and I owed that bastard for some of the things that he did to me. I led him on until he had a case of blue balls and then I walked away from him. As far as the pity and contempt is concerned, that's all in your head. You know I love you, baby, you have to know it."

"Yeah, Chrissi, that's why you didn't get in until five-thirty and why your cunt was soaking wet. And the way you treated me when you got here didn't seem much like love to me."

"What did you expect me to do? You called me a stupid bimbo and then you walked off and left me there. You know me, lover, and you had to know that there would be payback. I didn't get in till five-thirty because when the band quit I joined some other people and we went out for breakfast and then we talked and caught up on all the gossip."

She walked over to the dresser and got her purse, "as far as the wetness goes, it came out of here" and she tossed me a small bottle. It was filled with a milky white liquid and the label said, "Enhance Plus" and underneath it said, "A personal silicone lubricant."

"We passed a 24-hour adult bookstore on the way to breakfast and I stopped and got that stuff and squirted some in my pussy just before I came into the room. Now let's just stop all this foolishness and get in bed. Getting John all hot and bothered got me all hot and bothered and I need you to take care of me baby. I need it bad, so hurry baby, please?"

Chrissi was taking another shower following our rather strenuous workout on the bed and I was busy packing. I was almost done when I noticed the bottle of "Enhance Plus" sitting on the dresser. I picked it up to put in Chrissi's suitcase and I noticed something. The bottle was almost full – no more than a quarter inch missing. I know how much I swallowed the night before and it was a damned sight more than a quarter of an inch of stuff out of an eight-ounce bottle. Hell, the first gulp alone was more than what was missing from the bottle. I unscrewed the top and put some on my finger and licked it. There wasn't any taste to it at all. There had been more of a tang to what I'd tasted, a touch of saltiness. And then I noticed something else. I was standing there holding the open bottle and looking toward the bathroom when Chrissi came out toweling herself off. She saw me standing there with the bottle and I saw something pass over her face, something like, "Oh shit" or "Oh fuck me, he knows."

I screwed the top back on the bottle and set it down on the dresser.

"I wanted to believe you, Chrissi, I really wanted to believe you and you almost got me go for it. It would have worked if you had put this bottle away before I got a chance to take a good look at it. But there isn't any way that a quarter inch of stuff out of an eight-ounce bottle equates to the amount of stuff you pushed down my throat last night. And you should have read the label before trying to pull your stunt on me. I've eaten you after I've cum in you so I know what sperm tastes like, and what you fed me last night had the salty tang of cum." I tossed her the bottle, "Read the label, Chrissi. Especially the part where it says "clear, taste-free and odorless."

"Oh come on, baby, you're overreacting. You know that I love you and only you."

"Do I, Chrissi? I don't think I do. I think you loved having a husband who was a door mat for you. A husband who loved you so much that he turned a blind eye to all of your escapades and believed everything you told him, true or not. Yeah, I know you always told me what you did, but what you told me about was what you knew I saw you doing anyway. All you did was confess to what I already knew about and it's the stuff that I don't know about that is eating at me. I don't believe your story about what happened last night, Chrissi. You got fucked by John or one of your other old boyfriends, or maybe several of them, and then you showed me how much you loved me by forcing me to clean you out. Hubby just found his back-bone, Chrissi, and I'm out of here," and I picked up my bag and walked out of the hotel room.

End of the 2nd Story

The Relay

Her tongue lovingly licked the cock. It swirled around the bulbous purple head and I tingled in anticipation. I could feel her eyes on mine as her hot mouth opened and engulfed the head of the cock. It took all of my will power not to burst out of the closet and rush to the bed to claim what was rightfully mine. Instead, I sat perfectly still and watched as my wife of twenty years sucked the cock of one of my coworkers - a coworker who thought I was miles away on an overnight business trip. Nancy's head bobbed up and down while her fingers massaged his balls and before very long, Charlie grabbed her head in his hands and started thrusting up at her face. Nancy pushed his hands away, took her mouth from his cock and as I watched the saliva drip from her lips, she laughed and said, "Not so fast - not so fast!" She moved her body and swung a leg over Charlie, and holding his cock at the entrance to her body, she looked over at the closet as she slowly lowered herself onto the stiff pole. I ached for relief, but my hard cock had to be left untouched. I had promised I would not cum until I could take my sloppy seconds.

You might be asking how a staid old married couple could find themselves in such a situation. I was in my closet because a $13-relay failed at, depending on your point of view, either the right or wrong time.

Some background - Nancy is forty-two, has shoulder length silky brown hair, hazel eyes and a body that some would call either voluptuous or pleasingly plump. Whatever you call it, it had no trouble generating hard-ons in most men - especially in the men who gathered at our house one night a month for a poker game. The location had rotated from home to home and was usually held at our house once every six weeks, but for the past six months, due to such circumstances as divorce, death in the family, etc., there were only two of us who had enough room to host the game. As a result, the game was being held at our house every other week.

On game nights, Nancy would usually set up a snack buffet and then go out with her girlfriends, or to the library, or see a movie. When she left, I would usually pat her on the ass and say something like, "Tell whoever you pick up that he has to have you home by midnight," and she would chuckle as she went out the door. I thought I was being witty, but what I was doing was planting ideas in the heads of several guys who really wanted to fuck her. Looking back, I remember one night when I made such a remark after Nancy was gone one of the guys asked, "She doesn't really pick up guys, does she?"

"Why?" I had responded, "Don't you think she could?"

"Hell no!" he said, "She could get anyone she wants.

On the fateful night that changed our lives, Nancy did what she usually did. She covered the dining room table with a green table cloth, made a pot of coffee in the 30-cup urn, set out the snacks and checked to make sure there was enough ice on the beer. By the time all the guys had arrived, she was ready to leave. She kissed me on the cheek and said, "Win, baby, win."

I patted her on the ass and said, "Try not to hurt him too bad."

She gave the usual chuckle as she headed for the door, but that night, for the first time ever, she made a comment as she went out the door. Over her shoulder she said, "I'm not even sure his wife will let him come out and play tonight," and then she was gone. I saw the guy's exchange looks, but I didn't give it a thought.

About an hour into the game, the phone rang. It was my swing shift foreman calling to tell me that one of the presses had broken down in the middle of a critical run. Since I was the On-Call Manager for the weekend, I was required to go back into work and to try and solve the problem. I explained the situation to the guys and told them to play on, no need to break up a good game, but I probably would not be home before they left. It took me thirty minutes to get to work and as soon as I walked in the door, the foreman came up to me and told me he was just getting ready to call me and tell me not to come in. They had found a bad relay, replaced it and the machine was up and running again. I told him to have a nice weekend and I headed home.

Nancy's car was in the drive when I got home and I walked past it on the way into the garage to get some more beer. I was coming up the back porch step and I saw Nancy at the kitchen sink rinsing glasses. I was just about to open the door when I saw Norm come into the kitchen and walk up behind her, he had his cock out and he walked up behind Nancy, pressed his erect cock against her ass and reached around to grab her tits. Nancy laughed and said, "Harold! Stop that!"

Nancy thought it was me. Norm let go of her tits and pushed her forward over the sink as he lifted her skirt and all the while Nancy kept saying, "Stop that, Harold. Quit that."

Norm moved his knees between her legs causing them to spread. He pushed the crotch strap of her panties aside and positioned his cock to enter her, she must have been wet and ready because when Norm pushed forward, his cock met almost no resistance.

"Oh God, that feels good," moaned Nancy, "but stop it, honey, before your friends walk in on us."

Do not ask me why I didn't rush in and smack Norm in the mouth. Don't ask why I didn't just open the door and holler, "Hey! Stop that shit!" Don't ask - because I can't give you an answer. I don't know why I stood there and watched Norm fuck my wife any more than Nancy knew why she'd made the married man comment. All I knew is that I was frozen to the porch and my dick was getting very hard.

Nancy's feet were off the floor now and she was supporting herself by holding onto the sink. Norm had his rhythm going now and as he pumped in and out Nancy kept telling him to stop.

"Honey - you're going to embarrass me in front of your friends. Please stop baby, plea……oh, god that feels good."

Norm spoke for the first time, "Harold ain't here, Babe. Just me - good ole Norm."

Nancy cried out, "Oh god, no. No. You can't do this. Stop it stop it, put me down damn you."

"Sure I can. I am doing this. You came home early so obviously your married man couldn't get out, but don't worry, ole Norm can give you what you want."

Just then Dave walked into the kitchen, "Norm, what's keeping…Damn. I got dibs on seconds."

Norm turned holding Nancy by her hips while still thrusting into her. Nancy, her hands no longer on the sink for support, fell forward and her hands caught Dave's shoulders. While Dave stood there and supported her weight, he was busy pulling out his fast hardening cock.

Norm was apparently starting to push some of Nancy's buttons because she stopped pleading with him to quit and her cries turned into a series of moans, "Oh god, oh god, oh god, yes, yes, fuck me, fuck me."

By now Dave's cock was fully erect and he stepped back. Once again, deprived of support, Nancy fell forward bending at the waist. Dave caught her by her shoulders and her hands went to the front of his thighs. Nancy's face was only inches from Dave's cock and for almost a minute, she bounced on Norm's cock without moving her head, and then she slowly lowered her head and took Dave's cock in her mouth. Nancy rocked back and forth between them like a rag doll and then Dave said, "Let's get more comfortable. Let's take her over to that chair," and he pointed at a chair by the kitchen table.

Norm nodded ok and let Nancy down on her feet. Taking Nancy by the hand, Norm headed for the chair and Nancy meekly followed and when Norm pulled out the chair Nancy asked, "What are we going to do?"

Norm told her Dave was going to sit down on the chair and she was going to suck his cock while he fucked her from behind. While Dave was getting into position on the chair, Nancy removed her panties and placed her hands on the arms of the chair. When Dave was ready, she bent and her mouth engulfed his cock and it was at this point that my cock, which had been in my hand, erupted all over the screen door.

Norm stepped up behind Nancy, lined up his cock with her slit and drove into her just as Al and Sam came into the room.

"Jesus Christ, you guys. Why didn't you call us?"

While Al and Sam played with their cocks and argued about who would be next, Norm picked up his tempo and dumped his load into Nancy. He pulled out and Sam, who had apparently won the argument, took his place. The next to cum (not counting Nancy who had probably cum at least twice by this point) was Dave. He grabbed Nancy's head and started to hump up at her and I saw white stuff leaking out of the corners of her mouth. Nancy lifted her face from Dave's lap and as he started to get up, Al made as if to slide into his place. Nancy told him to wait and then told Sam to pull out so she could move. Next, she had Sam sit down on the chair where she straddled him and lowered herself down onto his cock; she motioned Al forward and as his cock approached her mouth she said, "God, I haven't done anything like this since college. I'd forgotten how good a lot of cocks can be." Her words were cut off as Al's cock slipped between her lips.

My eyes popped wide open when I heard that remark. Nancy and I had met in college. We had dated for over two months before she had even let me touch her tits. And all the while she was taking on a 'lot of cocks'? Boy did I ever feel stupid. Sam was the next to cum and he was followed shortly by Al. When Al pulled himself from her mouth, Nancy looked around, "Someone's missing. Where's Mike?"

"He went home an hour ago," said Al.

"Too bad. Maybe I'll get him next time!"

"Next time?" I thought, "There is going to be a next time?"

Norm said, "I'm ready to go again. Let's find someplace more comfortable."

Nancy said no. She said they had already pushed their luck and she needed to get cleaned up before I got home.

"When can we do this again?" asked Dave.

"Give me a couple of days," Nancy said, "and I'll call you and we can set something up."

That was my cue to get to my car and get it out of sight. I went to a local tavern and had a few beers and then called home to say I was on my way. "The guys still at it?"

"No," she said, "they finished and left."

When I got home, I came in through the kitchen and I noticed that the cum stains had been cleaned from the floor. Nancy was in bed freshly showered and as I came into the room, she threw off the covers and said, "I hope you are ready, Harold, because I am especially horny tonight."

As I slipped my dick into her, I wondered what a cunt full of cum was going to feel like, but she must have douched because I didn't feel a thing. I can't even begin to tell how disappointed I felt.

Three days later, Nancy told me she had a bridal shower to go to and that I shouldn't wait up for her. I debated as to whether or not I should bring up what I'd seen and challenge her 'bridal shower' story, but in the end, I didn't. The night went very slowly for me. I tried to read a book, but I couldn't stay focused on it. I turned on the TV, but it couldn't hold my interest. It seemed like every time I looked at the clock, only a minute or two had passed. I finally went to bed. Staring at the ceiling, I replayed the kitchen scene in my mind and I wondered how many she was with tonight. Surely those who had been at the poker game. Was Mike there this time?

I dozed off into a fit-full sleep. The closing of the front door woke me. I glanced at the clock - 4:27 a.m. Nancy came quietly into the room trying not to wake me and was startled when I sat up in bed.

"Sorry, Honey, I tried not to wake you."

I said nothing as I walked over to her, picked her up and carried her to the bed.

"Harold! What are you doing?"

I did not answer as I lifted her skirt and took in the lack of panties and the wet and matted cunt hair. I could see by her eyes that she knew I'd caught her.

"How many?" I asked. She made no reply and just looked at me with the look of a kid who had just been caught with his hand in the cookie jar. "How many?" I asked again. I could see tears welling in her eyes.

"I saw you in the kitchen the other night. You fucked four guys. How many tonight?" She started crying. "Nancy, there is no need for you to cry. Look at this." And I took her hand and placed it on my hard aching cock." "Is this the sign of someone upset?" I let go of her hand, but it stayed on my dick. "How many?" In a halting voice she said, "Seven."

"How many times?"

Her hand was now stroking my cock and with a little more assurance in her voice she said, "At least twice each. It was probably more."

I rolled over on top of her and as my cock found the entrance to her cum-soaked cunt I asked "Who?" She hesitated. "Who, Nancy? I want to know who!" I was starting to slowly fuck her and on each down stroke I asked, "Who?"

She started to respond. Her arms came up around my neck.

"Who?" as I drove down.

"Al" she said.

"Who?"

"Sam."

"Who?"

"Dave."

"Who?"

"Norm."

"Who?"

"Mike."

"Who?"

"Mike's brother."

"Who?" No answer. "Who?" Still no answer. "That's only six, Nancy. Who is number seven?" No answer. "Come on, Nancy. I have to know."

"Oh God, you're going to hate me. I'm just a stupid slut."

"Who, Nancy, who?"

"Alright damn you - it was the bell hop!"

"The bell hop?"

"Yes! The fucking bell hop. They ordered booze from room service and I fucked the bell hop for his tip!"

I fucked her until I was exhausted. I gave her a passionate kiss and then fell into a deep sleep. When I awoke, Nancy was next to me in bed, lying on her side, head resting on her elbow, just watching me.

"What now?" she asked.

"What do you mean?"

"I mean what now? What happens to us now?"

I looked at her for a moment. "What do you want to happen?"

"Nothing. I love you. The other night was an accident. It wasn't my fault!"

"I know" I said, I saw that you didn't start it, but when Norm set you down on your feet, you didn't try to get away. Nancy hung her head and weakly said, "I know."

"Tell me about it."

Nancy looked at me as if she was trying to make up her mind about something and then she took a deep breath. "Before I met you, I was the campus slut. My cousin took my cherry at eighteen and I found that I loved to fuck, anyone who could get a date with me had a sure thing. Then, one night at a frat party, I had too much to drink and I did it with two guys - at the same time. I loved it. Before long, I was the campus slut. Three, four, six - it didn't matter. I couldn't get enough cock. Then I met you. One look into your eyes and I knew you were the man I wanted to spend my life with. I stopped going out on dates; I wouldn't return phone calls; I turned down invitations to parties and I stopped going to my old haunts.

"I concentrated on being the 'little miss goodie two-shoes' I thought you wanted and I prayed to God that you would never find out what a whore I had been. The day you asked me to marry you was the happiest day of my life and since that day, I have not looked at, touched, or thought of another man. Until that night. It wasn't my fault. I tried to get away from Norm, but I had no leverage, and when he spun around and my head fell to the level of Dave's cock and I saw it there waiting for me a switch tripped in my head - it turned off Nancy the good wife, and it turned on Nancy the slut. I meant it when I said I'd forgotten how good a lot of cocks could be.

"What about last night?"

"I don't know. I honestly don't know. I did not intend to. When Al called and said they had things set up, I told him I was not interested. Then Norm called and said if I didn't go through with it, he would see to it that word got around about what I'd done. I told him to go to hell. The day before yesterday, Dave and Mike came by. Dave said he'd heard that I wasn't going to do them again, but they had all told Mike about what had happened and how I'd promised to do him next time. He said Mike had really been looking forward to it and it didn't seem fair that I let him down. Dave said if I would take care of Mike, he would see to it that the others didn't find out. I ended up fucking the both of them all afternoon. Yesterday I caved in to Norm's threats and you know the rest.

Unaccountably, I was rock hard again so I rolled over toward her and she opened her legs to receive me. As we fucked, I kept asking her questions, "Did they ask you to do it again?" No answer. "Did they ask you to do it again?" Still no answer. "Did they ask you to do it again?"

"Yesss," she hissed up at me as she had an orgasm.

"Are you going to?"

"No!"

"Do you want to?"

She turned her head away from me. "Do you want to?" Still no answer. "Do you want to?"

"YES!" she cried, "God damn you! Yes! Yes! I want to!" and she had her second orgasm as I pumped my sperm into her.

I rolled off of her and lay staring at the ceiling. "Well, we have established a few things here. One, you love doing it; two, you want to do it again."

"No!" She said, "I am not going to do it again!"

I turned to look at her, "Not even if I ask you to?"

She stared at me in disbelief. "You would ask me to do that? Fuck other men? I don't believe you. You can't be serious."

"Oh but I am. Watching you through the kitchen window that night gave me the most intense hard-on that I've ever had in my life. We know now that I want to watch you do it and we know that you want to do it. The only question now is, will you do it?"

She looked at me long and hard. "You really do want me to fuck other men while you watch?" I nodded my head yes. She came into my arms, "Ok baby, you want it - you got it."

I called and begged off of the next poker game and sent Nancy off to a 'bridal shower' on that night. My poker buddies have made several afternoon visits to my house while they think I'm at work, but I'm in the house watching. I have introduced Nancy to several business associates and co-workers at lunches and social gatherings and quite a few have managed to find their way into our bed. I've missed the last several poker games and somehow Nancy always has some where to go on that night. Nancy and I have talked about my becoming an active participant and someday I probably will, but for now, I am content with being a watcher.

End of the 3rd Story

Cruel Joke

She was, at worst, one of God's cruel jokes or, at best, a work in progress that he was pulled away from for something more important. She carried 125 pounds on a leggy five-foot-eight-inch frame that measured 38-23-36. Her long brown hair hung down to her waist and just the sight of her walking away from you could make you cum in your pants. Her tits were magnificent! Imagine a football cut in half - two stiff cones tipped with inch long nipples. She had everything that most women would die for - everything except for a face. This body straight from Heaven came equipped with a face straight from Hell; ache scars so bad that it looked like someone had stepped on her face wearing golf shoe spikes. And if that wasn't enough, an automobile accident left her with a scar that started over her left eye, angled downward across the bridge of her nose, crossed under her right eye and finished on her right cheek. So, naturally, the question on everybody's mind, the question they were too polite to ask, but you could see it in their eyes, was why had I married her?

That is a question easy to answer, but given today's attitudes hard to understand. I am from a generation that was brought up to accept responsibility for their actions. I got drunk one night, was carried away by lust for that magnificent body, took her virginity and got her pregnant, and here I am. When she miscarried, she expected me to pack up and leave - to end the marriage and get on with my life. But by then I had come to see past the outer shell and see the beautiful person inside. I discovered what a prize I had in Abby; intelligent, warm, caring, witty, and loyal and so I told her, "Sorry, but you are stuck with me."

Until that day, she had apparently looked on our marriage as one of convenience, and one I would get out of as soon as I could, and even though that is what she thought, she still did everything in her power to be the best wife a man could have. She was a better than average cook, a good housekeeper, and our sex life, while not great, was adequate. She treated sex as part of her wifely duties, but there was no passion, no fire. That all changed on the day I told her that she was stuck with me till "death do us part." She became a sexual forest fire - raging out of control and determined to burn me to ground. For six months, she tried to fuck me to death; at night when I got home from work, when we went to bed, and when I got up in the morning. And then one night, after months of trying to hold my own with her, and badly losing, I made what I thought was a joke.

"If you keep this up I'm going to have to get someone in here to help me."

Abby was licking my dick, trying to get me up again, and without looking up from her work, and in a calm voice she said, "Do you have anyone in particular in mind?"

I had not expected that response and for some strange reason, my dick twitched when she said it.

"Oh, I see we have pushed a button here. You want someone else to do me?"

My cock sprang to attention. She stopped what she was doing and looked up at me, "You do! You want someone else to fuck me. I'll be damned. My loving hubby is a closet pervert."

I rolled over and put my freshly erect cock to work. Later, as we cuddled, she asked how long I'd been thinking about her with another man. I told her that I never had, that my reaction had come as a total surprise to me.

"But what about you? You were pretty casual in asking me who I have in mind."

She pulled me tighter, "Baby, don't take this wrong, but I've thought about what it would be like with another man ever since my first time with you. You have to remember that you are my only experience. All the girls I went to school with, and most of the women I work with, sampled what was out there before settling down and getting married. Hell, if we both hadn't gotten drunk that night, I might still be a virgin. Don't forget, the guys were not beating a path to my door. I heard all the girl talk and it did make me curious about things."

"What sort of things?" I asked.

"Everything! The differences between guys, cock size, who were the better lovers, you know, the ones like rabbits that came quickly, and the ones who took their time."

"What else? I inquired.

"Stuff like the difference between white guys, black guys,

Latinos and Asians; what threesomes were like, what girl-girl sex was like, you know, all the stuff that sexually active teenagers talk about."

We were both silent for a while and then I asked her what she was most curious about. She thought for a moment before saying, "Just what another guy might be like."

"Curious enough to find out?" I asked.

Abby chuckled, "Get serious, lover. You got past the face, but no one else ever has."

"What if the face wasn't a problem? If we could find a way to work around that, would you still want to satisfy your curiosity?"

Abby stared at me for a moment before replying in an almost inaudible voice, "Yes!"

Several days later at work, I was sitting at my desk staring at the wall when my friend Bill walked over to me.

"What's up, Bud? You look like someone stole your favorite toy."

I smiled at him, "I'm trying to figure out how to be a pimp."

He laughed and said, "That needs an explanation."

So I spun him a tale, "I've got a very old and dear friend who has asked me to help her get even with her husband. She found out he is sleeping with his secretary and she wants me to find someone discrete to help her get even."

I could see the interest in Bill's eyes, "What does she look like?" he asked.

"Like a fucking wet dream. If she weren't so much like a sister to me, I'd do her myself. The problem is going to be finding someone willing to do it the way she wants it done." Bill made "give me more" motions with his hands, "She doesn't want anyone to know who she is so she is going to wear a hood or a mask. She will rent a motel room, give me the number, and I'll send the guy to her."

Bill said, "That doesn't sound too complicated. Where do I go, and when?"

I looked at him, "You serious?"

"You bet! I'm always looking for some strange and if she would have been good enough for you, she's good enough for me."

<<O>>

And so it was that two nights later, I sat in the family room trying to watch TV, but thinking about what was happening in room 136 of the Best Western Motel. Bill was supposed to be there at seven and at eleven I'd not heard from Abby so I figured all must have been going well. I kept looking at the clock, but the minutes just crawled by. At midnight, I took myself off to bed and fell into a fitful sleep. A car door slamming woke me and the bedside clock said four thirteen. I heard her come in and about five minutes later, she came into the bedroom. "How did it go?" I asked.

"Perfectly" she responded as she jumped onto the bed, "Oh baby, thank you, thank you, thank you for letting me do it" and her hand went for my cock. She felt wet and squishy as I entered her, which surprised me because I thought she would have showered and cleaned up before coming home. We fell asleep in each other's arms so I did not get the story until the next day. Bill had arrived at seven and she met him at the door in nothing but her mask and a pair of black "come fuck me" pumps. After a period of foreplay they had intercourse for about twenty minutes and then they rested and made small talk. Then Bill went down on her, they ended up in a sixty-nine followed by more intercourse. Another rest period, followed by a blowjob, followed by more intercourse after which they fell asleep. They woke up at one, fucked again and then they showered together which led to their fucking again. They dressed to leave, but Bill got turned on again watching her roll on her nylons so they fucked one last time. I was amazed - I didn't think Bill had it in him.

I asked her what they talked about during their rest periods and was surprised to find out that they had talked about me. Bill told her about how hard it was for me to be the one setting her up, us being so close and all, and he offered to do it for her in the future thereby relieving me of all the stress. He had given her his number and told her she could call him anytime. I wasn't too keen on that idea - I wanted to keep some control over things, but Abby thought it was a good idea, which brought about the question, "Are you going to do it again?"

Abby gave me a solemn look, "If you'll let me."

Over the next several months, Bill arranged for Abby to satisfy her curiosity on many things; she had several lovers, white, black, Latino and Asian; she had her first BI experience, and got to suck an uncircumcised cock. And, of course, she was fucking Bill on a regular basis. I began to wonder if Abby's curiosity was ever going to be satisfied, or if I was going to spend two nights a week for the rest of my life wondering what she was doing on those nights. I got a partial answer on a Thursday night. Tuesdays and Thursdays were the nights Abby usually went out so when I got home from work I did not give a second thought to her walking around the house in nylons, garter belt, and her high heels. I told her she'd better cover herself up or I was going to send her out freshly fucked. Just then the doorbell rang and she surprised me by going to answer it without covering up. I got an even bigger surprise when Bill walked in the front door and the two of them engaged in a passionate embrace.

Abby turned to me, "Tonight the curiosity is how it feels to take on two men at the same time. You up to it?"

I was speechless at seeing her with Bill without her mask on. Bill was the first to catch on. "Hell, Bud, when you told me the bit about the mask I was almost sure that it was Abby you were setting up. When she answered the door the first night and I saw those tits, I knew for sure. I told her to take the mask off, that I knew who she was."

It was a fantastic night. Abby got fucked in every way that it was possible for two men to do. As Bill was leaving that night, Abby said, "We will have to do this a couple of more times to make sure I didn't miss anything," and at that, Bill and I gave each other 'high - fives'. After he was gone, Abby turned to me and said, "You are really special. I hope you know that and that I love you to death."

I gave her a warm smile, put my arm around her and headed for the bedroom. "I've still got one more thing to try," Abby said, "Can you set me up a gangbang? Say five, maybe six guys?"

"Your wish, Baby," I thought, "is my command." I'd have to call Bill first thing in the morning and start working on it.

End of the 4ᵗʰ Story

Closet Guy

I have a thing for older women, more specifically, older married women. It started when I was sixteen and it continues to this day, some twenty odd years later. I guess it's fair to say that I got an early start sexually. I was playing "doctor" with the girl next door, Kay, when I was eleven and just before my twelfth birthday, I accidentally got to see my parents making love. Unfortunately Kay moved away shortly thereafter, but I still think of her and I'd like to think that she still thinks of me.

By the time I was eighteen, I had managed to get myself laid a dozen or so times, almost always by a girl a year or two older than me, but getting laid as a teenager, as I'm sure most of you know, is very hard work. The success rate is like one out of fifty tries unless you are lucky enough to have a Carol Meade (school slut), but the Carol Meades of the world are few and far between and they are always found on the arms of the older guys, guys who already have cars.

It was the summer of my eighteenth year and my best friend Tom, who lived just across the alley from me, and I were going to hop on the DSR and ride down to Briggs Stadium to watch the Tigers play the Orioles in a double header. I went across the alley and into Tom's back door (we did things like that back then - go into each other's house unannounced) and called for him. He didn't answer, probably couldn't hear me over the shower that was running, and so I headed back toward his room. He wasn't there so I figured that it must be him in the shower and so I headed for the bathroom. The shower stopped just as I got to the open bathroom door and I saw Tom's stepmother stepping out of the tub and onto the bathroom floor.

I'd seen several naked girls in the last couple of years, but I'd never seen tits like those on Mrs. Rose. She noticed me standing in the doorway and I expected her to scream and grab the shower curtain to cover herself, but instead she just looked at me and said:

"What's the matter, Dan? Never seen a naked woman before?"

The look on my face said it all.

"You haven't, have you? Well, I don't mind if you look at me. There is nothing wrong with nudity and I think that if you are comfortable with your body and with yourself you don't need to be ashamed. Why are you here?"

I stammered out about the ball game and she said:

"I thought Tom told you. He is spending a week with his grandparents. While you're here," and she tossed me a towel, "dry my back for me please."

I caught the towel and with trembling hands, I began to rub the water droplets off of her back. "Thank you," she said when I had finished drying her entire back and she turned around to take the towel from me and her breasts brushed against my arm. She either didn't notice or didn't care and she took the towel from me and walked back to throw it over the shower curtain rod. I watched that magnificent ass walk away from me and my dick was harder than I could ever remember and I knew that I had to hurry home so I could jack off. I started to turn and go but she said:

"Don't run off, I need you to do something for me," and she asked me to follow her. She led me to her bedroom and said, "Just wait a minute for me to throw a few things on. I'm going to need help with the zipper on my dress."

She sat down on the edge of the bed and rolled on her nylons, stood up and put on a garter belt and then stepped into a pair of high heels. She walked over to the dresser and bent over, digging through the drawer and leaving me to stare at that ass and her hanging tits. Her legs were slightly apart and I could see her hairy mound between them and I was hurting bad. I was torn between running for home and taking care of myself and staying to see as much as I could.

She stood up and turned, panties and bra in her hands, and walked toward me. Handing me the bra she said, "Here, hold this," and then she stepped into her panties. She took the bra from me and turned her back, "Hook me up," she said and as I stepped forward to do it, my hard cock touched the cheek of her ass. She spun around, bra dropping to the floor.

"Oh Danny, how stupid of me. I'm sorry, baby, I should have known better. It's all my fault. Here! Let me make it better."

She went to her knees in front of me and before it even registered on me what she was going to do, she had my cock out and in her hands.

"Oh it's a nice one! Much better than Tommy's and almost as nice as my husband's," and then she took it in her mouth.

I'm ashamed to say that I came almost immediately, but Mrs.

Rose had more surprises in store for me. She kept my dick in her mouth and swallowed every bit of my cum and she kept her mouth on me until I was hard again. She stood up and undressed me, led me over to her bed and for the next two hours, Mrs. Rose rocked my world. Finally she said:

"You have to go now, Danny. Mr. Rose will be home soon and I have to clean up. This is our little secret, right? You won't tell anyone about this, will you?"

"No, Mrs. Rose" I stammered, "I'll never tell anyone, honest."

She gave me a smile, "Good, you keep quiet about this, baby, and maybe we can do it again."

We did, many, many times over the next two years and after Mrs. Rose, there was no going back to girls of my own age. Mrs. Rose taught me a lot during those two years and I was a pretty accomplished lover when I went off to college. I was also a whole lot wiser about a few things. Remember her comment, "....yours is much better than Tommy's?" One day when I was busy pounding her pussy and we heard:

" I'm home!"

Mrs. Rose pushed me off her and rushed me into the closet and warned me to keep quiet. Tom came into the room. and said:

"Waiting for me I see."

Mrs. Rose said, "I'm always ready for you, baby, you know that," and then I got to watch the two of them bounce around on the bed and surprisingly enough I got a charge out of watching. When she made Tom quit, "Your father will be home pretty soon and I have to get cleaned up," and he was out of the room she came and got me out of the closet. As she led me to the bed she said:

"We have just enough time to finish what we started before I have to get you out of here," and I got my very first sloppy seconds. "You won't say anything about this, will you?"

I laughed and said, "And ruin what I've got going here? Not a chance."

She patted my cheek and said, "You are a sweet boy. We can talk about this tomorrow."

I stood in the closet and watched Mrs. Rose and Tom a couple of more times and Mrs. Rose always timed it so I could screw her one more time after Tom was done and before her husband got home. I always wondered if Tom ever stood in the closet and watched me, but if he did, he never gave any indication.

I owe Mrs. Rose a lot. I got three things from her that I carried forward into my life, a thing for older women, a desire to stand in a closet and watch, and the confidence and self-assurance that I needed to go after older women. In college, instead of chasing after the girls my own age, I haunted the malls and shopping centers looking for older women and I had surprisingly good luck in finding them. There are a lot of dissatisfied housewives out there if you know where to look and have the balls to approach them. Of course, you do occasionally have to put up with a crying baby, but to me it was always worth it.

I went all the way through college without ever screwing a girl my own age and my senior year was spent almost entirely in the company of a thirty-eight-year old divorcees. But I never got to watch from the closet while in school though, I think I may have been watched a time or two. I was surprised at how much I missed it.

It wasn't until I graduated that I got to watch from the closet again and it happened in a most surprising way. It was my mother's birthday and she and my dad had several people over for a party. I was talking to Brenda, an old and dear friend of my mom's, they had been sorority sisters in college, and she made the remark, "I never see you with a girl, Danny," and I replied "That's because young girls don't turn me on Aunt Brenda."

She wasn't really my aunt, but I'd always called her that. She asked, "What does turn you on?" and I said, "I'm into older women." "How old?" she wanted to know and I said, "About your age."

She gave me an odd look and we parted. About an hour later, I was coming out of the upstairs bathroom and I found Brenda standing in the hallway. I thought she was waiting to use the bathroom, but she grabbed me by the arm and pulled me across the hall and into the bedroom.

"Hurry," she said, "I can't be gone too long or Harry (her husband) will come looking for me."

She pulled me to the bed, stepped out of her panties and knelt on the bed. Being no fool, I unzipped, stepped forward and buried my bone in her waiting pussy.

"Oh god" she groaned, "That feels so good. Fuck me, Danny, fuck me."

It had been some time since my last piece of ass so I went at Brenda hard and fast. It took me about five minutes and I shot my wad and as she pulled on her panties she said:

"Thanks. I needed that. We will do it again sometime - soon!"

We had just started for the door and we heard someone coming, "It's Harry," she said, "He's looking for me," and she grabbed me and pulled me into the closet. We left the door open just enough so that we could see and the bedroom door opened, but it wasn't Harry who came in, it was my mother and she was followed by an old friend of the family.

"Hurry," she said as she closed the door behind them, "We don't have much time," and then Brenda and I watched as my mother repeated the same scenario that Brenda and I had just done. Brenda had my cock out and was stroking it as she whispered in my ear, "She always was such a slut."

I watched in fascination as the woman who gave me life showed me how I had been conceived. God, but it was one major turn on. When mom and her lover were gone, Brenda pushed open the closet door and moved in front of me and wrapped her lips around my cock. I came almost immediately. Brenda looked at me when she was done and said:

"Watching her really turned you on, didn't it?" I nodded a yes and Brenda said, "Want to watch her again?" I looked at her and wondered why she was asking and then I nodded my head yes. "Good, we can kill two birds with one stone. Call me in the morning," and then she left me there with my limp dick hanging out of my fly.

The next morning, I called Brenda and she asked me if I could come over and spend a good part of the day. Since I hadn't started job hunting yet, I told her that I could.

"Good," she said, "Try and get here between twelve and twelve-thirty."

I was there at eleven forty-five and Brenda let me in and took me straight to her bedroom. "You and I are going to have so much fun together, baby. I'm sure glad that you told me that you like older women."

Once in the bedroom, she stripped me and started sucking my cock. She was doing a simply marvelous job of it when the doorbell rang and she stopped sucking me and said:

"Oh good. That's them. Pick up your clothes and get in the closet. Be quiet now, we don't want them to know you are here."

I guess I must have looked confused because she said, "You'll like it, trust me on this."

Brenda's closet had louvers in the door so I was able to lean back against the wall and look out. It was only a minute or two before two men came into the room and started undressing. A minute later my mother walked into the room and I suddenly understood what Brenda had meant the night before when she said kill two birds with one stone.

I suppose I should be ashamed to admit that watching my mother (with Brenda's help) fuck those two guys damn near to death turned on something fierce, but I won't because I'm not - ashamed that is. It turned me on to watch her, but I had no desire to fuck her, even though Brenda did eventually get around to trying to talk me into it. When my mother and Brenda had milked those two guys of all they had to offer and they, along with my mother, had dressed and gone, Brenda came and got me out of the closet:

"I never asked your position on sloppy seconds," she said, and I gave her my answer by pushing her back on the bed and mounting her. Brenda and I began an affair that lasted almost three years. She got a big kick out of setting me up to watch my mother and occasionally herself bounce around on her bed with an assortment of different men and I got a kick out of it too.

My affair with Brenda ended when she introduced me to Megan. Megan was a divorcee about ten years older than I was and she was by far the sexiest woman I had ever laid eyes on. I asked her out, she accepted and we started dating. Even though Brenda is the one who put us together, for some reason, it pissed her off that we were spending so much time together, maybe because it cut down on the time I was spending with Brenda. About three weeks after I started dating (and fucking) Megan, Brenda called me on the phone and told me that I needed to be in her closet by one the next afternoon.

"You are finally going to get to see a gangbang."

She had been telling me since we started having sex together how big a slut my mother was, "And I'm not saying it in a mean way, lover, I'm as big a slut as she is," but one of the stories she told me about my mother I just refused to believe. She said my mother loved gangbangs, "The more the merrier. I watched her take on seventeen men one night. Of course I was taking care of the other nine, but I couldn't hold a candle to your mom. God, but that woman sure does love cock."

Like I said, I didn't believe a word of it so I guess Brenda decided that she had to prove it to me. I was in her closet at the appointed time and I watched as the room started to fill up with guys. I counted twelve of them before the bedroom door opened and Megan walked in. Brenda had set me up! I was supposed to watch Megan get totally fucked out and then never want to see her again. Well, it backfired on Brenda. I watched as Megan fucked those guys into the ground and my cock stayed rock hard the whole time. She sucked them, she fucked them, she did double and triple penetrations and when they all left she looked like she wanted more. I pushed open the door and walked into the room and she said:

"What are you doing here?"

"Long story," I said, "What's more important is what I'm going to do now," as I stripped off my clothes. I was going for the gold when Brenda opened the door and saw what was going on. The sudden realization that she had lost her gamble didn't stop her from coming in and joining us and it was a good thing that it was so late in the afternoon and Megan and I had to get out of there before Harry got home. There was no way in hell that I could have done those two women justice. Over dinner that night, I told Megan what I was doing in the closet and she knew right away what Brenda had tried.

"The bitch," she said as she laughed. "She wanted to keep you for herself. So tell me, did you enjoy watching me?"

I smiled and said; "I think the way I acted when I came out of the closet answers that question."

She gave me a contemplative look and said, "Do you think you could stand doing it two or three times a week?"

Without hesitation I said, "I would much rather participate, but yeah, I could watch."

That was eleven years ago. Megan and I are married now and I get to watch her from the closet several times a week, usually only one or two guys, occasionally three, and sometimes I get to join in. It depends a lot on who it is she is fucking. If it is one of her clients (she sells Real Estate) I don't get to, but if it is just somebody she picks up, I get to join in. She does one gangbang a month and I'm not allowed in on that. For some reason, the guys invited to play have to think I'm out of town. Once or twice a month I get to go and see Brenda and she still sets my mother up for me to watch. She has never stopped trying to get me to have sex with her, "I'll make her wear a blindfold - she'll never know!" but I'm satisfied just watching.

I did get to see her do a gangbang - eleven guys - and it was awesome, a real turn on. I sometimes wonder if my dad knows what is going on. If he does, it doesn't seem to bother him and he and my mother seem very happy with each other. It just could be that he knows about my mother what I know about Megan, there is just no way that one man will ever be able to satisfy her. I don't know about my dad, but I'm getting all I can handle and I don't mind in the least watching Megan give the rest away.

End of the 5th Story

The Project

She was hot! She was hot and she knew it. The table had been 'guy central' as guy after guy made the pilgrimage to the shrine to ask for her to bestow even the smallest amount of attention on them. She danced with a few, but turned three times as many away.

Some things never change.

She was hot! She was hot and she knew it. The two girls with her weren't bad, but they didn't even come close to her. A steady stream of guys made their way to her table and after a moment or two of conversation, she sent them on their way. Football players, baseball players and all of the other types of jocks wanted to sit with her at her table in the school cafeteria, but she turned them all away.

I sat and watched and wished I had the nerve to try, but if she wouldn't have anything to do with the school's elite what chance did a bookworm like me have. None I thought; not a chance in hell. Bobby the bookworm. That was me. The kid with the worst case of acne on the planet. The kid who sat in the back of the class room. The shy guy who kept to himself.

Two years went by and Bobby the bookworm had filled out some. The acne had faded, but my face was so covered with scars and pits that it looked like a golfer with spiked shoes had walked across it. I was still the shy guy and I still sat in the school cafeteria and looked across the room to the table where she sat with her two friends and held court.

And then the strangest thing happened. She looked my way, our eyes met and she smiled at me. I knew it as sure as I knew my own name. She didn't smile in my direction, she wasn't smiling as she looked off into space – she was smiling at me. The buzzer rang announcing the end of lunch period and breaking the spell and we all got up and shuffled off to our next class. I didn't have any shared classes with her in the afternoon so I didn't see her again until my first two classes the next day.

I thought I saw her glance my way once or twice, but I was probably mistaken.

I was sitting in the cafeteria alone at a table which is how it usually was when she and her two friends came through the serving line. I, along with every other male in the place, watched as she paid the cashier. Next she would look around for an empty table and we would all watch as she and her two friends walked to it. It was the walk that we all wanted to watch. It was the sexiest sight in the world. Even if you couldn't see the rest of the package the walk alone would give you the hard on of all hard-ons.

The cashier gave her the change and she looked around the room. There were several empty tables on the east side of the room and none on the side where I was sitting although there were three empty seats at my table. She turned and headed toward the empty seats at my table and behind her I saw her two friends look at each other in confusion before following along behind her. She walked up to my table, looked at me and said:

"May we join you?"

I was too stunned to say a word, but she knew the likelihood of my saying no was on a par with the moon being found to really be a big blob of cheese and so she sat down. She looked at me and said:

"Robert, right?"

I nodded a yes.

"So tell me, Robert, why do you sit here every lunch hour and watch me like a hawk?"

Her friends looked from her to me and then back to her and "what the hell is going on here" was as clearly on their faces as it was in my mind. I was shy, but it was the kind of 'shy' that prevented me from approaching people, not the tongue-tied kind of shy when people started talking to me. I smiled and said:

"Beauty attracts the eye. Extreme beauty attracts the eye and holds it."

She appeared surprised at that. The doofus was not a slack-jawed clown? I had no idea what she was thinking at that moment. I wasn't the kind of guy who was privy to the way a goddess thought. She gave me a dazzling smile and asked:

"If that is true why have you never come over to talk to us?"

"What? Me? A commoner approach the throne?"

She laughed and said, "We could stand a steady diet of that kind of flattery, right girls?"

Her two friends, Carol and Bev, gave half-assed smiles that clearly indicated that they had no idea of what was going on.

"Seriously" she said, "Why haven't you ever spoken to me before?"

"I can turn that back on you. We have been classmates for over three years now. Why haven't you ever spoken to me?"

"Because I am the queen bee and all the males are supposed to approach me, not I them," and then she laughed and said, "The truth of the matter is that I have been pretty much a superficial stuck-up twit. I'm so used to all of the good-looking guys fawning over me that I have never paid much attention to guys who look like you."

There was a sharp intake of breath from Bev and Carol when she said that and she laughed again and said:

"I'm the queen and the queen can say what she likes." She looked me right in the eye and said, "You know what you look like so you are not surprised that I see you the same way, right?"

I shrugged and said, "No, not really."

"Good. We start off with no illusions."

"Start off?"

"That's right bubba, start off. Meet me after school and you can carry my books home."

"Carry your books?"

"A figure of speech, Robert. I usually go out the east door."

Then she switched subjects to whom to vote for the prom king and queen and we talked while we ate lunch. When the buzzer went off she said:

"East door at three. See you there."

She walked off leaving me sitting there wondering what the hell had just happened. Befuddled yes, stupid no! At three I was on the steps outside the east door when she came out. Bev and Carol were with her and when they saw me waiting I saw the look that passed between them. Each was soundlessly asking the other "Do you know what is going on here?" There was no surprise on her face when she saw me because she knew that I would be there.

She handed me her book bag and I took it. At the bottom of the stairs she turned right, but I took her arm and steered her to the left. She gave me a questioning look and I said:

"Bear with me, my queen. All will become clear soon."

I walked us into the student parking lot and up to a 1993 Ford Mustang convertible. I unlocked the passenger door, opened it as I bowed low and said:

"Your chariot awaits, my queen."

None of the three had ever seen the car before which wasn't all that odd since I'd never seen it myself before the previous night. It was my eighteenth birthday, but the decision had been made that we would celebrate it on Saturday so I wasn't expecting anything until then. Mom had told me to take out the trash while she got dinner ready and dad got out the plates and utensils to set the table. I went out the door to the attached garage where the garbage cans were and stopped in my tracks when I saw the Sea Green Mist Mustang with the white convertible top. It had a huge red bow on it and a streamer that said "Happy Birthday, Rob."

I just stood there and stared at it. Mom and dad came up behind me. Mom said, "Happy birthday, honey" and my dad said, "The color is kind of yucky, but you're young enough that it can grow on you."

Mom punched him and said, "Shut up, you. It is beautiful and I'm pissed you didn't give it to me and give Rob my clunky looking van."

"Couldn't give it to you," dad said. "You go out driving in that and I'd be beating guys off of you with a stick and I'm too old for that shit."

Mom laughed and said, "You are kind of old a decrepit. Maybe Rob will loan it to me some night and I can go cruising and find me some stud who can keep up with me."

Dad said, "I'll show you old and decrepit," and he picked her up, put her over his shoulder and carried her in the direction of the bedroom as she laughed and told him to put her down.

I held the door so Bev and Carol could get in the back and then she climbed in the front and settled into the white leather seat while I put the top down. I started it up and turned to her and said:

"Where would my queen like to go?"

That was the start of my relationship with Melissa Anne Courtney.

<<O>>

She directed me to Bev's house and then to Carol's and told them that she would call them later. Once we were alone she said:

"Why don't we go through the drive-thru, get a couple of Cokes and then drive over to the park?"

"I hear and obey my queen."

She laughed and said, "I should have found you sooner."

"I've been here all along."

"Tell me about yourself."

"Nothing to tell. I'm a bit shy and I keep mostly to myself except for a half dozen really good friends. Mostly I go to school, study and spend time at the library three or four times a week."

"Why so much time at the library?"

"I belong to a chess club that meets there on Tuesdays and a book discussion group that meets there on Thursdays. Wednesdays I read books to a group of four, five and six-year-olds."

"I notice that you don't participate in any sports."

"Don't care much for them. I'm not into physical competition. I do play tennis with my mom on weekends and bowl with my dad sometimes, but I get most of my exercise in the gym that my dad set up in our basement. But enough about me. Why has the queen deemed this lowly commoner worthy of her attention?"

She was silent for a moment and just as she was getting ready to say something we arrived at the Burger Barn and pulled into the drive-thru. I ordered two value meals and then drove across the street to the park, got out and went to a picnic table and sat down. She took a bite of her burger and a sip of her Coke and then said:

"The truth hurts, Robert, but given the way you accepted my comment on your looks I believe you can handle it. I also said that I was a superficial, stuck-up twit and it is true, but I had never been aware of it. I didn't have to be because I was too busy being adored and fawned over. Boys have been flocking to me since I was twelve and I had my pick. If the one I picked turned out to be a toad so what? Just dump him and pick another.

"I never lacked for a date and I didn't have a care in the world and it might have gone on that way forever if I hadn't overheard a conversation between my mom and dad. I wasn't supposed to be in the house. I was supposed to be at a sleep-over at Carol's, but she got sick and so I went home. Apparently my parents didn't hear me come in and they were talking about me. My dad was worried about my future if I didn't change my ways. He commented that all of my boyfriends were empty-headed jocks and if you took the last five I'd gone out with and lumped all their brains together they still wouldn't be able to come up with the sense that God gave a grape. He said that they only reason that any of them spent any time at all studying was because they had to maintain a 'C' average or they couldn't play sports.

"My mom said it wasn't really that bad and besides I was young and having fun like you were supposed to when you were my age. My dad said that was true, but he was afraid I'd take my taste in boys with me when I went off to college this fall and I'd end up with some meathead whose only ambition was to play pro ball.

"I went up to my room and thought about what he'd said and I realized he was right. The only guys I had ever dated were good-looking jocks. A lot weren't as dumb as my dad depicted, but they were almost all interested in sports and it seemed like that was all they talked about. When I studied, it was never with the guy I was dating at the time; it was always with Bev, Carol or a couple of other girl friends. I tried to remember the last time I'd had a meaningful conversation with one of my boyfriends and I couldn't remember even one. My dad was right. I picked my boyfriends on appearance alone and it dawned on me that the reason I went through boyfriends so fast was that except for looks, they didn't have anything going for them that would capture and hold my interest.

"I thought about it for a couple of days and decided that I needed to see how the other half was. I looked around and there you were. This is the truth may hurt part. I wanted to get away from jocks. I wanted to get away from yummy looking hunks. I wanted someone who my daddy wouldn't think of as just another meathead and like I said, there you were. Even at that you were the luck of the draw.

"It was night before last that I finally decided to do it and I spotted you yesterday sitting alone at lunch and I thought, "Whoa, Lissa, there he is, the perfect guy. Not the best looking and not a jock and he is on the honor roll every semester so when I saw you sitting alone at lunch today, I headed for your table and here we are. So what do you think of your queen now?"

"So I am a social experiment?"

"Why don't we say that you are part of a project?"

"A project?"

"Yes. The project is to try and change the self-important, stuck-up superficial twit into something else. Are you up to the task?"

"Probably not."

She lifted an eyebrow at that and I said, "You said it yourself about four hours ago when you told me that you never paid much attention to guys who looked like me. The problem is that you are not the only girl with that attitude. I'm eighteen and have never been on a date with a girl and not from the lack of trying. I wouldn't have a clue as to what I could help you do as part of your project."

"You are pulling my leg right?"

"Not in the least. Never found a girl who wanted to go out with a guy whose face looked like it had been worked over by a cheese grater."

She sighed and shook her head. "Last week, Mellissa would have been one of them. I guess there are two projects to work on now."

"Two projects?"

"Yep. Me and you. You get to work on the re-invent Mellissa project and I get to work on the turn Robert into a social butterfly project. Maybe they will complement each other. Can you dance?"

"My mom made me take dance lessons when I was in the seventh grade."

"Done any since then?"

"With my mom at home. She and my dad used to compete in ballroom dancing events. When he is gone on business trips, she wants to dance to fill in her evenings."

"Okay then. The first step in what I shall refer to as the "Bobby Project" will be to get you out into the company of others on dates. The goal will be to have you ready to shine at the prom."

"The prom? I don't have a date for the prom. I don't even

know anyone I can ask to the prom. Every girl I have ever asked for a date has turned me down."

"Of course you have a date, silly. You just haven't formally asked me yet."

"You? You are going to be my prom date?"

"Depends."

"On what?"

"A silly little requirement known as "asking.""

I looked at her stunned and she said, "Repeat after me, Robert. Will you go to the prom with me, Mellissa?"

I stared at her in total confusion. How could this be happening? That the best looking and most popular girl in the school was sitting on a park bench and talking with me was mind boggling in itself. That she was telling me to ask her to the prom defied all logic.

"Come on, Robert, you can do it. Just follow along with me. Will you go to the prom with me, Mellissa?"

I pinched myself and felt the pain so I knew it wasn't a dream. I took a breath and asked:

"Miss Courtney, would you do me the honor of allowing me to be your escort to the senior prom?"

"I thought you would never ask. Of course I will. Now that we have that settled we need to go and see your mother."

"My mom? Why?"

"If she competed in ballroom dancing competitions, she knows how important it is for you to be in sync with your partner. We need to have her see us together so she can make comments and suggestions. As you point out Robert I am the queen and the queen will need to reign supreme on the floor at the prom. When would be a good time?"

"I'll have to ask when I get home."

She looked at me and I found that she was pretty good at reading facial expressions.

"What are you thinking Robert?"

"I find it hard to believe that this close to the prom the best looking and most popular girl in the senior class doesn't already have a date, but mostly I find it hard to believe that you want to go to the prom with me."

"I have been asked by a half dozen guys and I have put them off since I was having a hard time trying to pick among them. I've already told you why I've never dated any one guy for very long and all the guys who asked me were the same as the ones I kept changing. There were all cut from the same cloth; out of the same mold so to speak. Your senior prom is supposed to be special and I was hoping for something better to come along. Then I did the re-evaluation thing and here we are. As your queen, I'm going to lay a quest on you. It is up to you to see that your queen's senior prom is special. Accomplish this and your queen may grant you a knighthood or kiss you and turn you from a frog into a prince. Fail your queen and she may leave you a frog forever."

"I hear and obey my queen."

She laughed. "You big doofus. I should have checked out frogs sooner."

I drove her home and walked her to her door. She kissed my cheek and told me she would see me at school the next day.

Over dinner, I told my mom that I had a date for the prom and told her what Mellissa said about getting some pointers on our dancing and mom told me to bring her home with me after school. I called Mellissa and she told me she had no plans for that afternoon and that she was looking forward to dancing with me.

Mellissa and I shared two classes and they were both in the morning and at the end of the second one, she told me to make sure that I saved her a seat at my table during lunch. When I sat down in the cafeteria, I thought I saw people looking at me and I wondered what was up with that.

I found out when Mellissa and the ever present Bev and Carol joined me at my table. Mellissa had told the guys who had asked her out that she wouldn't be going to the prom with them. She told Carol, Bev and a few others that she was going with me and the school grapevine spread the word. After some small talk about what Mr. Anders had covered in third hour, Mellissa asked me if it would be all right if Carol and Bev could come with her to my house and I said that it was okay with me.

At three, I was waiting for them at the east door and we drove to my house. Mom and Mellissa seemed to instantly connect and after a bit of conversation mom said:

"Okay, you two; let me see what you got."

We went into the family room which had a hard-wood floor and mom put on the CD that we usually danced to and started it playing. The first number was a waltz and it became immediately apparent that Mellissa couldn't dance. I mean she could dance like most teenagers, but she wasn't up to ballroom dancing standards. I was making her look bad. Not at all what I wanted for my queen. Mom was not the soul of discretion. She flat told Mellissa:

"You need some work honey. Let me show you what it should look like."

She held out here hand to me and hit the play button again and I took mom around the floor until the tune ended. Then mom said:

"We need to do one of two things here. Either Bobby has to tone it way down or we need to bring you up."

Mellissa said, "I vote for bringing me up. How do I do it?"

"Hard work, honey. Hard work and time. How much can you give me?"

"Every minute I'm not in school. That includes weekends."

"What do we have? Two weeks until prom?"

Mellissa nodded a yes.

"Okay then. Every night after school and all day on Saturday. If we make good progress we can skip Sundays." She turned to me and said, "It means that you will be responsible for having dinner ready when your dad gets home. That all right with you?"

"No problem."

Mellissa said, "He cooks too?"

"My Bobby is a man of many talents. Sooner or later some very lucky young lady is going to realize what a catch he is."

I blushed and mom told me I wouldn't be needed for the day's lesson, but to be prepared to work hard the next day. As I headed for the kitchen, I heard Bev ask if she and Carol could sit in. I didn't hear what mom said, but I was pretty sure it would be okay with her.

As I drove the girl's home they talked about dresses and other prom related things and when I got Mellissa home, I walked her to her door. I got another kiss on the cheek and she told me to remember to save her a seat at my table next day.

I was late getting to lunch the next day and when I got there Mellissa, Carol and Bev were already at a table, but the fourth seat was occupied by Ray Hendricks so I found a seat on the other side of the cafeteria. That afternoon at three, Mellissa showed up at the east door alone and as we drove to my house, she apologized for not saving me a seat at the table.

"Ray sat down before I could tell him that I was saving the seat for you. He started talking to Bev about their prom date so I couldn't chase him away."

I shrugged and we pulled into my driveway. We were just walking into the house when I found out why Carol and Bev hadn't been with Mellissa when she came out of school. Ray pulled up in front of the house and he and Bev got out of his car even as Carol and Steve Miller pulled up behind him. I looked at Mellissa.

"Your mom said she would also work with Bev, Carol and their dates."

I just shrugged and said, "I guess the queen's court should look good too" and we went into the house.

Mom was in her element. She had to be a dance instructor just waiting to come out of the closet. She spent the afternoon going through the basics using me as a visual aid until about an hour before dad was due home and then I had to hit the kitchen and start fixing dinner. When dad got home, he worked with mom on the lesson and around six-thirty, things broke up and mom came and told me that Mellissa was staying for dinner.

Dad pretty much dominated the dinner table conversation asking Mellissa all about herself, her family, what she was going to study in college and what were her goals in life. When dinner was over, he said he would handle the clean up so I could work with mom and Mellissa. At nine, I drove Mellissa home and as soon as we pulled away from my house she said:

"Okay, Robert, give."

"What?"

"Why the long face earlier when Ray and Steve showed up with Bev and Carol?"

I was silent for a moment and then said, "I've spent most of my school years with girls having little or nothing to do with me and then my fairy godmother took pity on me and waved her magic wand. The fairy dust settled and there you were. That is the only possible explanation for it. And like the fairy godmother only gave Cinderella until midnight, I know that I am only going to have a short time with you and I guess I don't want to share what little time I will have with anyone else."

She didn't say anything to that, but then what could she say? She knew it was true. I walked her to her door and she turned to face me with a strange look on her face as she said she would see me at school the next day. She leaned forward and kissed me. Not on the cheek, but on the lips. Then she turned and went inside.

When I got home, dad said that he would order pizza for the next day's dinner and then take over the kitchen chores on Saturday to give me more time to work with Mellissa.

"I think you got a good one there sport and we need to do what we can to see to it that you keep her."

"Yeah! Right" I thought. Like that could ever happen.

<<O>>

Friday at lunch, all the talk was about dancing and prom dresses and my only part of the conversation came when I was asked what dances I thought were likely to be played. I said it was more than likely that half would be waltzes and the rest fast numbers based on current popular tunes and I speculated that there would be at least one each tango, cha-cha and samba.

"Do we have time to learn those?" Carol asked.

"Maybe some of the basics" I replied.

Of course that night, Carol had to bring it up and equally, of course, mom took it as a challenge.

"How hard do you want to work?" she asked. "We can work late tonight and then a full day tomorrow. You will need to be here Sunday most of the day and next week work a couple of hours later than we have been. We have tonight, all of this weekend and all of next week and weekend. I think we can do it, but you won't have time for much else."

I could tell that Ray and Steve were not all that interested in doing it, but Mellissa, Carol and Bev were all for it so Ray and Steve got dragged along. It was either that or possibly losing girlfriends thirteen days before the prom. We worked until ten before calling it a night and then I took Mellissa home. We were almost to Mellissa's house when she said:

"Your queen is pissed."

"And what pray tell has this lowly one done to upset his queen?"

"We haven't been on a date yet. We have spent all this time together and have yet to go on a date."

"This lowly one apologizes, but at the risk of incurring the wrath of his queen he must say that it was the queen who made the decision to fill up all of her available time with dance lessons."

She looked at me for a moment before saying, "I guess I did, didn't I?"

Before I got to her house, she told me to take a left on Jerry Street.

"Why are we doing that?"

"Be patient, you'll see."

She had me make a right on Paris and I looked questioningly at her because Paris was a dead end. At the end of the block, she told me to pull over and park. I did as she said and then she said, "Get in the back" as she got out on her side and moved to the back and I followed.

"It doesn't look like we are going to be able to squeeze in a date before prom and I'll be damned if I'm going to wait thirteen more days to do this. We can't do it up front because of the bucket seats, center console and gear shift so we will have to do it back here. Kiss me."

I was going to argue? She broke the kiss and said, "You weren't joking when you said there hadn't been any girls in your life were you? If there were, they sure didn't teach you how to kiss. Here, let me show you."

And she did. After a couple of minutes she said, "Not bad, but we will have to spend some time working on it," and then she sought my lips again. It was another half hour before she told me that it was time for me to get her home. The goodnight kiss at her front door was a little on the intense side and I drove home giving my fairy godmother effusive thanks. It might not last long, but I was going to have some very nice memories.

The next ten days took on a sameness. We spent twelve hours a day on Saturday and Sunday working under the task master that my mother had become. Monday through Friday was school and then after school, four more hours of lessons. The following Saturday and Sunday were also twelve-hour days. Each night when I drove Mellissa home, there was a make-out session. Sometimes I got the feeling that Mellissa was waiting for me to do something, but I didn't know what.

When I got home after taking Mellissa home following Sunday's session, mom told me that she thought that Mellissa and I were almost good enough for competition.

"You've always been ready, baby, but Mell does need just a little more work. Carol would be too if she had a better partner, but I'm sorry to say that Bev and Ray don't have what it takes. They will shine at the prom, but that will be because most of the other kids won't have had the benefit of lessons."

"You really think that we are that good together?"

"You bet, baby."

I went to bed that night feeling pretty damned good.

That good feeling was with me right up until the end of fourth hour. At the end of our second hour class, Carol asked me to meet her outside the east door before going to the cafeteria for lunch and then she took off for her next class without giving me a chance to ask why or even agree to meet her. Curiosity being what it is I was there waiting when she came out. She walked up to me and hesitated. She wanted to say something, but it seemed she either didn't know what to say or how to say what she did want to say. I tried to help.

"Go ahead, Carol. As you might imagine, I'm used to hearing bad things from girls. I can handle it."

She took a deep breath and then she said, "Mell is my best friend and I usually don't butt into her business, but over the last couple of weeks, I've discovered what a great guy you are and what a great family you have. I don't want to see you hurt, Rob, but I'm afraid that Mell is going to hurt you. I know why she is spending time with you, but I know her, Rob. I know that you aren't the kind of guy who will hold her interest for long. She is using you to satisfy some need she feels she has and then she will drop you like she has a dozen others.

"I see the way you look at her, Rob, and I know how you are going to feel when it happens. I guess I hoped if I prepared you for it that it might help some."

"I appreciate your concern, Carol, but I'll be okay. I've always known that it wouldn't last. At least I will have had prom and that is something that wouldn't happened before Mellissa took an interest in me for whatever reason."

"That brings up the other thing. You do know that you will only be able to spend part of the prom with her right?"

"What do you mean?"

"She is bound to be elected prom queen and Dick Harbor will more than likely be named prom king and they will have to spend some time together. Then there is the queen's court and tradition says that she has to dance with all the male members of her court."

I shrugged and said, "At least in the record books, I will have been her date and our picture will be in the class year book. That is something I'll always have. Come on, were late for lunch."

That night after our dance lesson, I drove Mellissa home and as soon as I pulled out of the drive Mellissa said:

"I saw Carol talking to you today. What was that all about?"

I hesitated and she said, "Come on, sweetie, you can tell me. Carol and I are too tight for whatever you tell me to affect us."

"She says she likes me and doesn't want to see me hurt."

"So?"

"She more or less told me not to let myself get too close to you."

"Why would she do that?"

"The idea was that if I didn't get too close it wouldn't hurt as bad when you dumped me and moved on to your next conquest."

"And you think that is going to happen?"

"Given my history with the opposite sex why wouldn't I? You are the queen and I am a lowly serf and we lowly serfs know better than to try and climb too high."

"Pull over."

"What?"

"Pull the fuck over!"

I'd never heard a profane word from her so I was shocked, but I did pull over next to the curb. She turned and climbed over the center console and shift lever, turned off the ignition and then she kissed me. The kiss turned into a hot make out session. She lifted her sweater, grabbed my right hand and put it on her breast and then she placed one of her hands on my hard cock and rubbed it.

"I've never done this with any other guy. Not one of the studs and hunks I've dated have ever gotten this. You are special Robert and you are my guy. You are stuck with me asshole so get used to it!"

It was a nice thought for me to carry around even if I didn't believe it.

<<O>>

Tuesday and Wednesday went by quickly and it was prom night. My mom had picked out the corsage and she handed it to me as I started to leave. I was headed for the garage to get the Mustang when my dad said:

"Where are you going?"

"To get my car."

"Your ride is out in front."

I went to the front door and saw a stretch limousine sitting at the curb. He handed me two one hundred dollar bills and said, "Have fun." When I got to Mellissa's house and she came down the stairs to greet me she was so beautiful that I almost lost my breath. If I didn't get to experience anything else I at least got to see that vision walk toward me.

I had to pose for pictures as Mellissa's mom took twenty or thirty shots with her camera and she told me that she would make a set for my mom as I walked Mellissa to the door.

"You might want one of my queen getting into her chariot" I said as I opened the front door and Mellissa walked out onto the porch and saw the limo.

"Hopefully it won't turn into a pumpkin before I get you home."

Mellissa turned and kissed me with a kiss that made me weak in the knees and her mother got a shot of it.

"Would you please make me a thousand copies of that one" I asked and her mother laughed.

All eyes were on us as we walked in. Half of those watching were probably thinking "What the hell is she doing with him?" and most of the males present were drinking in her beauty and wishing they were me.

Mellissa, Carol, Bev, Ray, Steve and I dazzled the rest of the attendees as we dipped and swirled around the floor. Mellissa was indeed installed as Prom Queen and Carol and Bev ended up as part of her Court. The biggest surprise was that Dick Harbor didn't make it as King. The honor instead went to Mike Ashell who was one of Mellissa's old boyfriends.

The biggest shock of the night came when it was time for the King and Queen to dance. Mike had this big grin on his face as he walked up to Mellissa while the band started playing a waltz. The smile disappeared when Mellissa reached up, took the crown off his head, walked over to me, placed it on my head and then led me out onto the dance floor.

Just the two of us, alone on the floor with every eye in the place on us. If we had been in a dance competition during that dance we would have swept the floor with the other contestants. We were that good together. When the music finally stopped Mellissa and I bowed to each other as the place erupted in thunderous applause. I found out later that the band leader played the waltz an extra three minutes because we were doing so good he didn't want to stop us.

Mellissa took the crown from my head and took it back to Mike and then led him out onto the floor for the next dance. Carol walked up to me, elbowed me in the ribs and said:

"Show off. My turn now."

I danced with Carol, Bev and several other girls that night because there was no way I could keep Mellissa to myself for the entire evening, but I did have her for more than half the night.

There were one or two other highlights. When the band played a cha-cha mom's students were the only ones out on the floor and when a half hour later they played a second one mom's students each grabbed a partner from the crowd and led them out onto the floor and tried to lead them through the dance. The same thing happened when the band played two tangos. The first was just mom's crew and the second was mom's crew pulling partners from the crowd.

During the second tango I pulled Nancy Neubert out onto the floor and as I tried to lead her through the dance she said:

"Damn Rob. Where the hell have you been hiding?"

I almost laughed in her face. I had asked her for a date at least a half dozen times since we were in ninth grade together and she had always shot me down. I just smiled and kept my mouth shut.

The last dance was a waltz and all was well with my world as I moved around the floor with Mellissa in my arms. As the last note faded she kissed me and said:

"You are a frog no more my Prince."

My reverie was broken as she sat down beside me.

"Having second thoughts?" she asked.

"Not at all. Just thinking back to the senior prom."

"I could tell. That's why I asked you if you were having second thoughts."

"Not a one. It was just a paving stone on the walkway that led us here."

"More like two or three."

"Want another drink?"

"I don't think so. I told the sitter we would be home by eleven."

"Okay. I just need to make a quick trip to the bathroom."

When I came out I saw Mellissa talking to Carol. Carol said something and Mellissa laughed and then Bev said something and Mellissa laughed as Carol stuck out her tongue. They all hugged and I marveled at a friendship that had lasted for over eighteen years; from the sixth grade until now. I've had friends and good buddies galore, but I couldn't think of even one that I've been as close to as Mellissa, Bev and Carol were to each other.

I walked up and put my arm around my wife. "Goodnight all" I said as Carol and I turned and walked out of the Landing Strip Lounge and headed for home.

End of the 6th Story

Dating Shelly

Shelly looked at herself in the mirror as she applied her lipstick. She smiled at what she saw, "No wonder the guys have been hitting on you girl" she thought to herself. She stood five feet one and had one hundred and five pounds distributed on a 34-22-32 frame. Green eyes and long brown hair completed the package. She took one last look at herself in the mirror and thought, for at least the tenth time, "You shouldn't be doing this girl" but then she shook the thought from her head and headed downstairs to wait for Greg to pick her up.

Shelly knew she was good looking. Boys had been sniffing after her since her fifteenth birthday. But she knew it wasn't her good looks that had her popularity at an all time high right now. No, the guys were sniffing around her now because she was married and her husband had been gone for three months and could be gone for another six months to a year. The conventional wisdom, at least among the guys, was that as a married woman used to a steady diet of sex and now deprived of it because of a missing husband she would be getting desperate and if the guys played their cards right some one would get lucky.

The truth was that she was indeed desperate for sex, but she had promised herself that she would be faithful to Ralph while he was off answering that idiot Bush's call to arms. Shelly saw no reason for Ralph and his reserve unit to be in Kuwait. No one she knew believed that we had any business messing around with Saddam Hussein while things were still not settled in Afghanistan, Al-Qaida was still on the loose and Osama bin Laden still had not been found. But then it didn't really matter what anybody thought because the bottom line was that Ralph was gone and would be for quite a while yet and that presented Shelly with a bit of a problem.

Shelly was not a 'stay at home' type of person. While not necessarily a party animal she did prefer the company of others to sitting at home and watching TV or staring at the walls. For the first two months that Ralph was gone she had stayed home and behaved herself. She had spent every day at work fighting off the passes from the guys she worked with and most of her evenings saying no to Ralph's "friends" who wanted to look in on her and see if there was anything they could do for her while he was gone.

Finally, after two months of going crazy in her house alone she had said yes when one of the guys at work had asked her out. She had made it very clear right up front that it was going to be a platonic evening - dinner, dancing, a few drinks - with absolutely no hanky-panky. She'd had such a good time that she had allowed him to kiss her goodnight and that kiss had turned into a ten minute necking session that had her so hot when she got into the house that she'd had to use her dildo to get herself off. The fact that she had been able to put a stop to things before they had gotten too far along convinced her that she could handle things and she had started going out on a lot more dates. It wasn't right and she knew it, but giving away kisses was something she did freely underneath the mistletoe every year and it hurt no one. Besides, her husband would never know.

Then word got back to Shelly that she was considered a 'cock-tease' because she would date, neck a little, and then walk away leaving her dates all hot and bothered. The fact that she was left just as hot and bothered never seemed to occur to anyone so one day Shelly had a little meeting in the company lunch room with the six guys she had been dating and she had laid it all out for them.

"I'm married and you all know it. The fact that I prefer not to stay home and stare at the walls and so I date does not change the fact that I'm married. I've told each and every one of you before I went out with you that nothing was going to happen so you have no bitch coming. I don't mind a little necking, but I am going to stay faithful to my husband. So, if you can't handle that then stop asking me out."

This of course had the opposite effect of what Shelly had expected. The guys accepted her little speech as a challenge and were now more than ever determined to get into Shelly's pants. They even formed a pool, each placing two hundred dollars in it with the man being the first to score walking away with the twelve hundred dollars. The result was that Shelly was asked out even more often. The guys had also noticed that the more alcohol they could get into Shelly the longer the make out sessions lasted and the feeling was that sooner or later the longer necking sessions would lead to Shelly's downfall. The next half dozen dates seemed to support their theory. A couple of guys managed to get their hands under her sweater and play with her tits and one guy even managed to get a finger in her pussy before Shelly shut him down.

And then Shelly found out about the pool. At first she was

pissed, but the more she thought about it the more she thought that she should teach the assholes a lesson. If they thought she was a cock-tease before wait until she got done with them now. The first one to feel her wrath was Ted. He had taken her out for drinks and dancing and was surprised when halfway through the necking session he had gotten a hand inside her bra and she had placed a hand on the bulge in his trousers and squeezed it a couple of times. He had gotten a finger in her pussy and finger fucked her for a minute or so before Shelly had pushed his hand away and said, "I'm sorry, I can't. It wouldn't be right" and then she pulled away from him and ran into her house.

The next one was Mark. He had his tongue down her throat and had gotten two fingers in her pussy and she had moaned and squirmed. He unzipped himself and pulled out his hard cock and had put one of Shelly's hands on it. She had stroked it half a dozen times before pulling away from him and running into the house. Then Charlie, George and Bob fell victim to her with Bob, her last date, getting so far as having Shelly jack him off until he came in her hand. The only problem with all she was doing was that she had managed to work herself up to the point where she needed to be laid in the worst way and she had come to realize that there was no way she could wait for Ralph to come home and take care of her.

Her date with Glen had gone smoothly. They had dinner and then went dancing and when Glen had pulled into her driveway they had started necking. It progressed to where Glen had her bra off and he was licking her nipples while she jacked him off. Shelly had pretty much decided that Glen was going to be the one who got to go all the way when he took his mouth off her left breast and said:

"You know you want it Shelly. When are you going to break down and give it up?"

For some reason the way he asked the question pissed her off and she said, "Never! As long as you boys have that pool going I won't do anything. I'm not about to give any one of you assholes bragging rights."

Glen grinned at her, "Fuck the pool. I won't tell any one if you don't."

Shelly had never thought that she would be doing what she was doing now. She had never planned on going to bed with anyone other than her husband, but there was no doubt about what her body wanted right then and after all, Ralph would never know. She would find someway to make it up to him when he got home. She was on her knees between Greg's legs and her hands were stroking his cock. She licked her lips and then she leaned forward and placed her lips on Glen's cockhead. Glen moaned and Shelly sucked him slowly and leisurely while caressing his balls and teasing his ass with a finger. After several minutes Glen groaned and said, "I'm going to cum baby" and Shelly drove her mouth down on him and clamped her lips tight as she felt Glen's cock throb and then explode into her mouth. She gulped and swallowed as hard as she could to try and capture all of his fluid, but some still managed to escape and drip down her chin.

Gradually Glen became soft, but Shelly kept her mouth on him and licked and sucked until he was hard again. Glen took her arms and lifted her up and then laid her back onto the couch. He leaned forward and kissed Shelly and his tongue probed her mouth as she felt the head of his cock pressing at her pussy. She spread her legs as far apart as she could to make it easier for him and she gasped in pleasure as he penetrated her. Shelly had orgasm after orgasm as Glen fucked her. She screamed in pleasure and begged him to fuck her harder and harder. When he finally came Shelly held onto him tightly as he drained into her body and then he fucked her two more times before the two of them fell asleep.

Shelly woke up to find Glen with his face buried in her pussy. Shelly loved to have her pussy eaten and what he was doing amazed her. Her husband had never eaten her pussy when it was full of cum, but Glen seemed to have a voracious appetite for his own juice and finally Shelly could take it no more and she pulled away from him and swung over him so she could suck his cock while he licked her pussy. Then they had fucked two more times and then showered together which led to one more bout on the bed. As Glen was dressing to leave he had asked if he could see her the next day and Shelly had told him no. "I can't play any favorites baby. It's bad enough that I cheated on Ralph; I can't compound it by taking on a steady boyfriend. You have at least five guys in front of you before you can come back."

Monday at work Shelly looked up to see the six men whom she had been dating come in to her office. Bob handed her an envelope and

Shelly looked inside to see that it was full of twenty-dollar bills. She looked up at the six men and Bob said, "Glen told us what you said about nobody getting anywhere as long as the pool was in place. We decided to give it to you so you could buy stuff for yourself from a place like Victoria's Secret. We aren't going to give up and it would be nice if you had on some real sexy under things when one of us finally gets lucky."

Shelly stared up at the six men torn between swearing at them for thinking that they were going to get what they wanted and wanting to take all of them on right then on her desk. Finally she put the envelope with the money in it in her purse and then she took a pen and a piece of paper out of her desk drawer and wrote on it. She tore the paper into six strips and then scattered them around on her desk. Then she looked at her six men and asked, "Who has the least company seniority?"

Bob was the junior man and she told him to pick up a piece of paper off of her desk and then she had the others do the same in order of inverse seniority. When they were done she asked, "Who drew number one?" Charlie raised his hand and Shelly said, "You're my date for tonight. Plan on eating in. Who has number two?"

Glen raised his hand and she told him he was tomorrow's lucky man. "Anyone have any questions?"

She looked around at the six smiling faces, "No? Then get out of here so a girl can get back to work."

As the door closed behind them Shelly smiled to herself. With six of them rotating she shouldn't get emotionally attached to any one of them, but if the number was larger she could be even surer. She wondered which one of Ralph's friends would be the next one to call her asking if there was anything he could do to help while Ralph was away. She made a mental note to stop and buy condoms on the way home.

End of the 7ᵗʰ Story

The Cock Report

"Joey, can I ask you what sounds like a silly question?"

"Sure, as long as you don't mind silly answers."

"No Joey, I mean the question is going to sound silly coming from me, but I really want to know the answer."

"Okay Aimee, shoot."

"Do all black men have really huge dicks?"

"Jesus Aimee, how in the hell should I know that?"

"Well, you did play sports in high school and college and you were in the Army for three years so I know you have been in a lot of shower rooms with other men."

"Yes, but I didn't spend my time in those shower rooms measuring cocks."

"But surely you must have noticed something?"

"Sorry baby, but checking out dicks just wasn't my thing. What's this all about anyway?"

"Judy says that black men have bigger dicks than white men."

"Well, there you have it. That slut would know if anyone would."

"She's not a slut Joey."

"She has had four husbands and every one of them divorced her for infidelity. She has spread her legs for damned near every man we know and that behavior more than meets the definition of slut as I understand it."

"Joey, she is still my best friend so please don't talk about her like that when you are around me."

I wondered if Aimee would still talk like that if she knew how many times Judy had tried to get me between her legs.

A couple of days went by and one night at dinner Aimee asked, "Can I ask you for a really huge favor?"

"I suppose. What do you want?"

"The next time couple of times you go to the gym for your work out would you see if maybe you could get a look at a couple of black cocks for me?"

"Good God Aimee, what is it with you and cock size all of a sudden?"

"I just want to find out if Judy is right."

"Why?"

"Because I'm curious. You know me Joey, I'm a screaming liberal. I'm out there marching with a sign and protesting like hell anytime there is even a hint of racial injustice. I've always said that blacks, whites, Latinos, Asians or whatever are all the same except for the accident of skin color. Now Judy is telling me that I'm wrong, that there are major differences between the races, that all blacks have bigger cocks. I don't want to believe Judy. We all have to be the same regardless of skin color. I have to know Joey, and I can't go find out for myself. Please Joey, I'm not asking you to take a tape measure with you, just a quick glance and tell me what you see."

She worked on me all the way through dinner and into dessert and I finally broke down and told her I would see what I could. I didn't mean it of course, there was no way that I was going to try and scope out cock sizes in a shower room. But even though I wasn't going to snoop in the shower I was going to try and get an answer for her. One of my good friends at work is black and I offered to buy him lunch if he would answer a few stupid sounding personal questions for me. I told him what was going on with Aimee and asked him right out if it was true.

"I wish I had a dollar for every white woman who has asked that question, but the answer is no. If you randomly select five hundred white men and five hundred black men you would probably find the same statistical variance in each group. If there were ten very large cocks in the black group you would find nine, ten or eleven very large cocks in the white group. The same could be said for medium sized cocks and small cocks; the percentages would be damned near the same. Your wife's friend probably only sees large black cocks because that is what she goes looking for."

"How would she find just big ones?"

"She only has to find one on her own. There are more white women out there who want to experience a big black cock than you might believe and like anything in our free market society if there becomes a demand for something someone will find a way to supply that demand. If a white woman finds one black man with a larger than average cock you can be sure that he has made it his business to find others. For some reason black men are hard wired in the brain to want white women so the propensity among black men is to share the white women they get. I'm not talking gangbanging here. Joe meets Mary who is curious about black cock. Joe does Mary and then calls up Bill and tells him that he has a hot white chick who likes black cock and I'll turn her over to you if you have something to trade. Bill puts Joe in touch with Jill and it just goes on like that. Judy could very well have seen a dozen big dicked black studs if that is what she was looking for."

That night when I got home Aimee asked me if I had seen anything that she might be interested in knowing. I told her that I'd seen a few things, but that I was going to watch for a week or so to get a good sample. Over the next two weeks I went to the gym seven times and on the seventh day I came home I told her that statistically there was no difference between the black race and the white race, at least in the cock department. I told her I had seen three large black cocks and four white ones about the same size, eight black and eight white ones about the same size as mine, and two small black and three small white ones. I could see the relief on her face and I said, "Press on Liberal Lady; fight racial injustice secure in the knowledge that we are all just folks with different skin colors."

A couple of months went by and I began to notice some things. Aimee seemed to be quieter and she spent a lot of time seeming to look off into the distance. We didn't talk as much at the dinner table as we used to and a couple of times I came home from work to find her lying on our bed crying. When I asked what was wrong she would just say that she wasn't feeling well. Our sex life started to slack off. From five and six times a week to four and then two or three and then two weeks without any and always the same answer, "I'm just not feeling well Joey." Then one night I came home from work to find a note on the kitchen table:

"Joey, I love you, I really, really do, but I can't live with you any more. I'm sorry,

Aimee

Frantic, I called her mother, her brother, her two sisters and anyone else I could think of to se if anyone knew where she might be, but no one knew a thing. Finally I thought of Judy. I called her and she said, "She's here Joey, but she doesn't want to talk to you."

"Why not?"

"She has her reasons. Not good ones as far as I'm concerned, but they seem to work for her."

"What the hell is going on Judy? She can't just walk out on me without a word, without telling me what is wrong. What the hell did I do?"

"You didn't do anything Joey. She did and it is killing her."

"Come on Judy, give – what the hell is going on?"

"Look Joey, I like you, I like you a lot. I think you are one of the nice guys, but I can't tell you a thing. You will have to get it from her. I will tell you this though, and don't you dare let her know you got it from me, but she plans on going to the house tomorrow to get some clothes while you are at work."

I called in sick the next morning, went out and moved my car around the block and then I went back into the house and waited. It was a long wait and I was starting to think that Judy had given me bad information when Aimee's car pulled into the drive. I moved to where she couldn't see me until she was well into the house and I could get between her and the door. Aimee came in the front door and went straight up the stairs and into our bedroom. I gave her a minute and then I followed her up. I went into the room, closed the door and then sat down on the floor with my back to it and waited to be noticed. Aimee backed out of the closet with an arm full of clothes and turned to drop them on the bed and then that's when she saw me. "What are you doing here?"

"I live here."

"That's not what I mean. You are supposed to be at work."

"I wasn't feeling good so I called in sick."

"Have you called the doctor?"

"It's not that kind of not feeling well. I got some news last night that kind of put me down in the dumps."

"Oh, I see," she said and she turned and dropped the clothes.

"What is going on here Aimee?"

"Please Joey, I don't want to talk about it."

"Unfortunately for you Aimee, I do, so you are going to have to whether you want to or not."

"Joey, will you just please leave. Don't make this any harder on either of us than it has to be."

"I'm not leaving Aimee, until I know what this is all about, and neither are you. There are only two ways out of this room, through the window or through the door, so unless you plan on jumping out of a second floor window the only way out is through the door and I'm not moving until you talk."

"Please Joey, I don't want to talk about it, it will only make things worse."

"Worse for who Aimee? How can it be any worse for me than it already is? The woman I love walks out on me without a word and I'm supposed to sit here with an over-active imagination to try and figure out why? I'm supposed to sit here, stare at the walls and think all kinds of things like maybe you left me for another man? You left me for another woman or you didn't leave me for anyone else, you just can't stand me any more? Then I could go way out there and imagine you over at Judy's taking part in orgies'" and when I said that I saw Aimee wince.

"That's it. I can see by your face, that's it. Judy finally corrupted you. That's why our sex life died; you are getting all you need over at Judy's. That's probably the real reason for your interest in the size of black cocks, right? You were trying to talk yourself into trying a couple and stupid me was your point man. Is it just one black man you are leaving me for, or is it a herd of them? Have you become as big a slut as Judy? Never mind, I don't really want to know the answer to that."

I got up from the floor and left the room. As I was heading down the stairs I heard Aimee call out, "Wait Joey, don't go" but I continued on down the stairs and left the house.

I got in my car and headed into work. I hadn't been there an hour when I got a phone call from Judy.

"You asshole! What did you do to her? She's over here bawling her eyes out and I can't get her to stop."

"Whoa up there lady. How did I get to be the bad guy here? I come home to find that she's left me. I was at the house when she got there and she wouldn't talk to me and so I left the house and came to work. That makes me an asshole?"

"Okay, so I'm sorry I called you an asshole. She wouldn't talk?"

"Not a word."

"It isn't my place to do this, but if she won't then I guess I'll have to. Buy me lunch at Anton's and I'll fill you in."

She was already there when I arrived and as I walked up to the table I thought, and not for the first time, about how sexy she looked. I suppose that might have had something to do with her being such a cock hungry slut. If you got hit on as often as she probably was it would be easy to get laid as often as you wanted. She had already ordered drinks and there was one sitting there waiting for me when I sat down. She pointed at it and said, "You need to hurry sweetie, I'm on my third and you might need to play catch up. A few drinks in you might make this go easier."

I took a sip of the drink and then set it down. "No games Judy, just tell me what the hell is going on."

"You haven't heard my terms yet sweetie. Do you want to know bad enough to take me home with you and give me a taste?"

"Yes, I want to know that bad, but no I won't. Is that what this little meeting is all about? You trying to get me in the sack?"

"No sweetie, but you can't blame a girl for trying. I've always wanted to see what it is that is so special about you that Aimee never shuts up about you."

"Maybe you can ask her now that she doesn't care any more."

"Don't even think that for a minute sweetie. Aimee loves you as much now as she ever did. She just can't face you. Your wife was bad sweetie, very, very bad, and now she has a guilty conscience.   She betrayed you and the thought of having to face you every day after what she did is tearing her apart. She has managed to convince herself that you would be better off with her not around."

"Just what is it that she did that was so bad?"

"She got laid sweetie, not just once, but several times and not by just one guy either."

"Aimee?"

"Yes sweetie, Aimee got herself fucked by seven different guys over a three day period and when it was over she hated herself for being so weak and abusing your trust and now she is beating herself up over it."

"You let that happen to her?"

"No sweetie, I just didn't stop it. Why should I have? I thought it was what she wanted. I thought that she had wanted it for a long time, but wasn't going to do it until you did it first."

"I'm sorry, but you lost me on that one."

"Sweetie, I'm a cock hungry slut and you know it. I'll fuck anyone who has a cock attached to him. I make no apology sweetie; I am what I am and what's more I love being what I am. Aimee is my best friend and I've known her a hell of a lot longer than you have. Do you really think that given how close I am to Aimee that I would try to hustle her husband behind her back? No way sweetie. Aimee pointed me at you and turned me loose."

"I don't believe you."

"Believe it or not sweetie it is still true. Did you know that your wife considers you a bit of a tight ass? One day I was asking her what was so great about being married to you and she said to me, her exact words sweetie, "Why don't you take him to bed and see for yourself. He could use a little loosening up." I said, "You wouldn't mind?" and she said, "Hell no girlfriend, it would only be sex and I know he loves me." That's when I started taking shots at you and I honestly thought that what she was really after was a chance to go out and play a little on the wild side, but she needed you to stray so she would have an excuse. It turns out I was wrong about that. She honestly felt that you needed to loosen up a bit and she wanted her best friend to do it rather than some stranger. So, when Aimee let loose I thought it was just because she got tired of waiting for you to go first so I didn't do anything to stop her."

"So just what exactly is it that she did?"

It had happened when I was out of town on a four-day business trip and it was just after I had given Aimee the cock size report. She and Judy had spent the day shopping and then they had stopped at a lounge for a few drinks and then they had gone back to Judy's and had several more. Then Judy had suggested that Aimee should be getting along home and Aimee had asked why Judy was in a hurry to get rid of her. Judy told her that Tyrone, her current boyfriend, would be there in about thirty minutes and she didn't think that Aimee wanted to be around when Judy rode his huge black cock. That led to a conversation on cock size and Aimee told Judy about my little survey. Judy told Aimee that I didn't know what I was talking about. More talk and a couple of more drinks and suddenly Tyrone was there and Judy drug him into the conversation. He of course said yes, all black men have larger cocks than white men. A couple of more drinks and then Judy said she would settle it once and for all and she made a few phone calls.

An hour later there were five black men at Judy's place and Judy had them all strip and stand in front of Aimee. The smallest cock in the bunch was nine inches and the biggest had been twelve and a quarter. Aimee sat on the couch looking from one to the other and shaking her head in amazement. Judy had grabbed Tyrone by the hand and had taken him into the bedroom and when they came out twenty minutes later it was just in time to see one man get off of Aimee and another one get on. Judy had no idea how Aimee had let it happen, but it was obvious that Aimee wasn't being forced. The men had picked Aimee up and had carried her into the bedroom and then she and Judy had spent the rest of the night being rotated among the men. The next morning Judy woke up to a crying Aimee, torn with guilt, upset over what had happened and at a loss as to how could ever face me again.

To cheer Aimee up Judy took her shopping again and again they stopped at a lounge for drinks only that time they stayed until closing and Judy had allowed them to get picked up by two black men. Judy's intention had been to drop Aimee off at our house and then take the two black men back to her place, but when they got to our house one of the guys asked if he could come in long enough to use the bathroom. They stuck around for a drink or two and then they all ended up in bed together. In the morning Aimee had said, "Well, I've fucked up my marriage and my life, but at least I was able to disprove a myth. Both those guys had cocks half the size of Joey's."

They had gone shopping again and that night had gone to Judy's place where Aimee had attempted to drown her sorrows with alcohol. Tyrone showed up and a little latter a couple of the other men from the first night had shown up and it turned into another group grope on the bed.

"The next morning Aimee went home and as far as I know she hasn't seen another man since. I do know that she was a big hit with the guys and they keep after me to bring her back. I know that several keep calling her and asking her to go out and that she always says no."

"So what do I do now?"

"Depends on what you want sweetie. Are you a big enough man and do you love her enough to forgive her or is this something that would always be between you and eat at you if you got back together?"

"I don't know the answer to that one Judy. I honestly don't know."

"Well sweetie, answering that question is the first step in deciding what you are going to do."

"What do you think I should do?"

"You are asking me that? The girl with four ex-husbands? That's a little like asking Attila the Hun for advice on setting up peace talks."

I suffered through a very bad three days. I talked to Judy every day to make sure that Aimee was okay and on the third day it occurred to me that I wouldn't be talking to Judy if I didn't care about Aimee. The next step was to admit to myself that I loved her and was miserable without her, but I was also honest enough with myself to admit that I did know the answer to Judy's question. What Aimee did would always be between us and it would always fester like a picked at sore. I spent another two days beating my head against the wall trying to figure out what to do. The only thing I could think of was shaky at best, but it was all I could come up with so I called Judy.

"What you thought Aimee wanted, do you think it would work in reverse?"

"What work in reverse?"

"You thought she wanted you to bed me so she would be free to play. Would our going to bed now have the same effect? You know, the old "You did and now I did and so we are even?"

"Oh no sweetie. It might work, but not with me. Six weeks ago I would have jumped at the chance and been in your bed in a heartbeat, but not now. Aimee is an emotional mess and I'm not going to risk my friendship with her on a maybe."

My only shot and it was shot down. Suddenly I knew what I had to do. It was a long shot and if it didn't work Aimee and I were history. I picked the phone back up and called Judy again.

"Remember how that first night happened?"

"Yes."

"I want you to take Aimee shopping again.

When Judy answered the door she said, "Are you sure that you want to do this?"

"I have to do it. If I walk away Aimee and I are toast. If I go through with it I at least have a fifty-fifty chance we can save things."

"On your head be it sweetie."

"Did it work?"

She led me to the bedroom, stepped aside and said, "See for yourself."

On the bed a very naked Aimee was on her hands and knees and being fucked by a black man while two other black men stood by the bed watching and waiting their turn.

"It took a lot more booze that I thought it would, but it worked. That's Tyrone in the saddle and the other two are Sam and Wendell. They all know what the score is, good luck."

On the bed Tyrone said, "Next up get ready, I'm almost there."

"That would be me," I said as I started shedding clothes.

Judy walked over to the other two and took them by the hand, "Come on. I'll do you guys in the living room and you can come back for some of her later."

Tyrone gave a grunt as he drove into Aimee and spilled his seed in her cunt and then he moved out of the way and I took his place. I pushed my cock into her as hard as I could and then I said, "First time I've ever gotten sloppy seconds from my wife."

She twisted her head and looked back at me and cried out, "No, you can't, you can't see me like this, oh God, not like this."

"Too late my little cock crazy slut. I'm already in and I'm not leaving until I've cum in your whorish cunt as many times as I can. If you can gangbang black men you can damned sure fuck your husband. At least he loves you for more than your pussy."

She kept crying, "No, no, no" and trying to get away from me, but I wasn't going to go anywhere until the night was over. Eventually the "No, no, no," turned into "I'm sorry, I'm sorry" and then the "I'm sorry's" turned into the sounds that I had grown used to hearing during our nine years of marriage – "Oh yes, oh yes, oh God yes." From then on until I fell asleep exhausted I took turns on my wife with the other three men.

When I woke up in the morning I heard Aimee and Judy whispering.

"You have to do it."

"I can't Aimee, you know I can't."

"Please Judy, do it for me please? Somebody has to do it or I'll never feel right. He showed me that he loves and will forgive me by what he did last night, but I still have to forgive myself. I've had others and he hasn't. Take care of that for me, please?"

"What should I do?"

"He loves to wake up to a blow job. When he gets hard climb on top and ride him and he'll take it from there. Keep him here all day and all night."

"What are you going to do?"

"Go home and get ready for his home-coming."

I heard footsteps leave the room and then a hot mouth captured me.

That was five years ago and as far as I know Aimee hasn't touched a cock other than mine since that night at Judy's although on occasion, when I've pissed her off, she mutters something about calling Tyrone. When she does I just say, "Tell him to bring Judy with him" and things seem to mellow out. Five years ago I wouldn't have given us a chance in hell of still being together, but we are and I think our marriage is stronger than it has ever been. Proof, at least to me, that love can find a way if you are willing to try.

End of the 8th Story

Darlene Does Them All

Platinum blond hair, ruby red lips, skin the color of California sunshine and the body of a porn queen - it was love and lust at first sight, on my part anyway. On her part? I doubt that she even noticed me; she was very, very busy at the time.

Mike, one of the guys I work with, asked me if I could give him a ride home from work one night. Since I had to drive right past his place on my way home anyway I said sure and we headed out. When we pulled up in front of his place there were two cars in the driveway and Mike said:

"I've got two roommates and it looks like they beat me home. Want to come in for a beer?"

Not having anywhere that I needed to be, or having anything that I had to do, I said I'd love a beer and I followed him into the house. As we walked into the living room I saw Darlene for the first time. She was on her knees in front of a very large black man, her head in his lap with her lips wrapped around his cock. Her head was moving up and down almost in time with the in and out thrusts of another black man who was fucking her from behind. The man sitting on the couch looked up as we entered the room and said:

"Hey Bro," (I don't know if I mentioned it, but Mike was also black) "Get your clothes off and get over here. This bitch is hot for black cock. I don't know if she'll do your buddy, maybe white dick don't do nothing for her. What about it honey, you do white guys?"

Darlene raised her head from his cock, turned and looked at me and said, "As long as the three of you give me all you've got, I'll fuck him," and she turned her attention back to the cock she had been sucking.

Like I mentioned earlier, it was love and lust at first sight. Given the 'lust' part you would have thought that I would have been out of my clothes in a New York minute, but somehow I knew that keeping my clothes on was the thing to do. Instead, I got a beer from the fridge and sat down to watch as Mike and his roomies fucked Darlene six ways from Sunday. She sucked their cocks and they fucked her in her ass and pussy; at one time she had all three of them in her and her moans and groans of pleasure had me rock hard. Mike called over to me:

"Hey man, you're missing one great piece of ass here. You sure you don't want to join in?"

I both surprised and stunned myself when I said, "No thanks. That's the woman I'm going to marry and I want to wait until at least our first date before we make love."

Mike's face broke out in a big grin and he laughed out loud, "Yeah! Right!"

The funny thing, I suddenly realized, was that I was dead serious.

It was three a.m. and Mike and his buddies had stumbled off to bed leaving a totally 'fucked out' Darlene lying on the couch. After about ten minutes she finally sat up and looked around. Seeing me still sitting in the chair and looking at her she asked: "What kind of flake are you?" I shrugged my shoulders and she went on, "You watch me being a total slut for three black dudes and you say you are going to marry me?"

I shrugged again, "What can I say? I saw you and knew that you were the one meant for me."

Darlene laughed, "God, but you sure are a piece of work. Why didn't you join in? You some kind of racist? Don't want to dip your wick in a puddle of black sperm?"

I told her I could hardly be accused of being a racist, after all, I was in the house as a guest of Mike's, wasn't I? Then I said:

"If the only way I can have you is to be the caboose at the tail end of a train of blacks, so be it, but I want my first time with you to be after a legitimate date. The usual, dinner, dancing, a kiss goodnight when I drop you off after the date and maybe you invite me in. It might not be the first date, or even the second, but I want to romance you before we make love. After that, we'll see."

She laughed at me again, "Honey, what you just saw is the real me. I'm fond of dark meat and lots of it, but I'm also an equal opportunity slut. I'll fuck anything male I can get and whenever I can get them. I am not a one man woman and I never will be."

I just smiled at her and said, "We will see."

<<O>>

Our first date was two days later and when she came to the door and found me standing there with a dozen roses she just shook her head and said:

"I can't believe I'm doing this, I just can't believe it."

Our second date was two days later and our third the night after that. On the third date Darlene invited me in and we made love for the first time. For me, it was fantastic, and I had the personal satisfaction of making her orgasm twice, something, given her preference for multiple partners, I wasn't sure I could do. When I asked to see her again the following Friday she told me that she couldn't see me because she had some people coming over. She told me I was welcome to stop by, but that we wouldn't have any time for ourselves.

She was right about that! When I got there a black guy let me in and told me Darlene was in the back and he pointed the way. I found her with three guys, all black, and the three of them were filling her three available holes. For the second time I watched as she took on everyone present. Four hours later the men were gone and Darlene was left lying on the bed with cum all over her magnificent body. She looked me in the eye and said, "You once told me you would be willing to be the caboose at the end of a train. Now's you're chance. You can fuck me or you can eat me, but if you ever want to see me again it will have to be one or the other."

I did both.

For the next three months I was Darlene's 'steady boyfriend' and we dated three or four nights a week. At least twice a week on those dates I had to watch as she let herself be fucked by a variety of different men in groups of anywhere from three to seven, mostly black, and when she was finished with them she would always look at me and ask, "Do you still want me baby?" And when my answer was always yes she would always say, "Then get over here and eat me or fuck me." At the end of our first month of going together I began asking Darlene to marry me and she always said no. She said that she couldn't be faithful to me so there was no sense getting married. I kept after her and eventually I wore down her resistance and she agreed to become my bride, but only on the condition that I understood ahead of time that she was still going to fuck other guys whenever she felt the urge. I know she threw that condition at me thinking it would make me shy away and the surprise was evident on her face when I agreed to her condition and told her to set a date.

The wedding took place on the third weekend in May and Mike

was my best man. It took a lot to convince him to do it since he believed that I was out of my fucking mind (his exact words) and should be committed. The wedding was a small affair, only twenty people or so, and it was held in my backyard. It was not your usual run of the mill wedding. To begin with, Darlene arrived at the house in a van with three black guys and it was obvious to anyone who saw them get out of the van that she had done them all on the ride over, and probably more than once. Two hours before the ceremony she fucked Mike and both of his roommates and twenty minutes before the "I do's" were said she gave the minister a blowjob. When the minister said, "You may now kiss the bride" I could taste him on her lips.

And then things really got raunchy. Before I took Darlene to our marriage bed she took on every male guest present and twenty-one cocks emptied in her that night and she was still moaning "next" when the last one left. She fell back on the bed and then she giggled and said, "Do you still want me baby?" I signified my yes by starting to undress. She watched me disrobe and when I was naked she spread her legs for me and said, "God, but you are one sick puppy. Come here baby, fuck me or suck the cum out the whore you just married."

Darlene and I have been married eight years now and things have changed just a little. Darlene decided she wanted to have a baby so she stopped fucking guys for three months because she wanted to make sure that I was the father. On the day she found out she was pregnant she celebrated by inviting over some of her favorite lovers and she fucked them all until they couldn't get it up anymore. From that night until the end of her eighth month she was back to being her usual self, fucking anyone she could get her hands on, and then she quit until the baby, a little girl, was six months old. She is down to one gang bang a week now, and dark meat is still her favorite; she does three blacks for every white, Latino, or Asian that gets into her and I am still the caboose that follows at the end of the train. I never get tired of hearing, "Do you still want me baby?" and seeing her spread her legs for me. My answer has always been, and will always be "Yes!"

End of the 9th Story

Connie's Birthday Present

I guess the first thing I need to say is that I never had any desire to watch my wife with another man, at least not when this started. What I did want was to give my wife a gift; something she had never asked for, something that she had never indicated that she wanted, but something I wanted her to have.

Connie and I have been married for almost fifteen years now and for me they have been happy years. I love her as much, if not more, as I did on the day I married her and as near as I can tell she feels the same about me. Our sex life is great and our desire for each other has never slackened; we go at it five or six times a week and two or three times a night is not uncommon. I work afternoons and Connie will occasionally get horny waiting for me to get home and on those occasions she will call me at work during my lunch break and we will engage in phone sex.

One day, on my way home from work, I stopped at an adult bookstore and bought Connie a couple of dildos so she would have something to use besides her fingers when we were on the phone. Both of them were larger than my cock, considerably larger in fact, and Connie laughed when she saw them, "I'll never be able to get those in me," but of course she did, and for the next seven months we put those imitation dicks to good use. It was probably there all the time and it just took me seven months to realize it, but during our phone sex Connie had gotten much louder when she had her orgasms. Her moans started earlier and lasted longer than when we had intercourse and then one night I found out why. I had pulled a muscle in my back at work and when I got home Connie was her usual horny self, but because of my back I was unable to perform. I grabbed one of her dildos and went to work on her with it and she went nuts on me. It was the size of the fake cock that was doing it to her and it was then that I began to seriously think about giving her the pleasure of the real thing, a real one that was at least as big as her toy.

Now you don't just have a thought like that and the next day go out and do it. First, you have to talk yourself into doing it, and it really wasn't all that easy even though it was my idea in the first place. All kinds of thoughts bounced around in my head. How do you find a guy with a big dick without coming across like a pervert or an idiot? What about the possibility of disease; of the man having a big mouth and telling all his buddies? What if she liked it so much that she became dissatisfied with me and just wanted bigger and bigger cocks? If I get past all that, how do I go about getting her to do it, or at least broach the subject to her? But I loved her enough to want her to have the pleasure so I set out to find out how to get it done.

The first order of business was to find a candidate for the job and I started my search at the same place I bought the dildos (dildi?). I bought several swingers magazines and read them cover to cover and while I found several guys with large cocks, I either didn't like the tone of their ads or I didn't like their looks. I bought a couple of more magazines, but with the same result. After two months of pouring over every magazine I could find I was at wits end, I could not find anyone that I could accept (Connie might have liked a whole bunch of them, but I wasn't at that point yet). Just when I thought my cause was hopeless a prospect was dropped into my lap. Connie and I were at a cocktail party one night and a couple hours into it I went out onto the patio for some fresh air. It was a cool, crisp night, the sky was clear and the stars looked spectacular. I moved off the patio to get away from the light so I could get a better view of the stars and I was standing there gazing upwards when three women came out onto the patio. They apparently did not notice me off to the side in the dark and so I inadvertently got to listen to their conversation.

"Did you hear about Toni and Darren?" said one.

"No" replied the other two, almost in unison.

"Well, Darren broke things off with her. Apparently she was pushing for marriage, but Darren told her he wasn't ready to settle down, but Toni kept pushing so he dropped her."

"Poor baby" said one of the other two, "I'll bet it killed her to give up that hunk of salami."

"What does that mean?" asked the third woman.

"Didn't you know?" replied the first woman, "Darren is hung better than most horses."

"How do you know that?" asked the third woman.

The first woman snorted and said, "Lets just say that Darren and I were real close at one time."

The third woman said, "Well don't keep us in suspense, just how big is he?"

"Well", said the first woman, "I put a tape to him once, and depending on which is the right place to measure from, he is either ten and a half or eleven and a half inches long and as big around as my wrist."

The third woman asked, "Why on Earth did you let him go?"

The first woman laughed, "I didn't. I pushed for marriage and he dumped me just like he did Toni."

There followed another five minutes of conversation during which the three of them compared the cock sizes of their husbands, boyfriends and lovers and then they went back inside. Interesting, I thought. So Darren had a big cock. I'd known him for over twenty years and I'd not known that. As an added bonus Darren and Connie seemed to like each other and I'd seen the way Darren looked at her. I doubted that I would have any trouble enlisting him in my plan, and I was comforted by the knowledge that Darren seemed to cut and run whenever anyone tried to nail him down into a long-term relationship.

Next I had to figure out whether to approach him first or sound out Connie first. I finally decided to get with Darren first because it would be easier to go back to him and say that Connie had shot the idea down, than it would be to go back to Connie and say Darren wasn't interested (what woman would want to hear that a man she had agreed to sleep with didn't want her?). Another week was spent in deciding how to approach him. I decided that the best way to do it was to be blunt and so I called him and asked him to meet me for a beer. I met him after work one night and after a few minutes of small talk I said:

"I understand that you just broke up with Toni. Is there another lady in your life yet?"

He gave me a "what the hell is this" look before saying, "No one at present. Just playing the field right now. Why?"

"Because" I said, "I want you to fuck Connie."

He was just taking a sip of his beer and he choked on it. After a couple of moments of coughing he said, "You what?"

"I want you to sleep with Connie" and then I went on to explain how she responded to the dildos and that I wanted to give her the experience of a real large cock as a birthday present. He stared at me in disbelief for several moments and then he started to laugh.

"This is a first for me. Most husbands lock their wives up in chastity belts when I'm around. You really want me to make love to your wife?" I nodded a yes. "A man would be a fool to turn down a chance at Connie. How do we go about it?"

I told him that I didn't have a clue, but that her birthday was coming up soon and he should plan to be available for that night. To plan on a romantic evening on me. I told him I'd pick up the tab for dinner and dancing and then I jokingly said I'd even pay for the condoms. "Deal!" he said. Now all I had to do was get Connie to agree.

How do you go about telling your wife that you want her to let another man get between her legs? I had no doubt that she would enjoy it, at least once Darren was inside her, but how to get her to agree to do it? How do you broach the subject? I needn't have worried; it was a piece of cake. The next evening at work I got a phone call at lunchtime. It was Connie, horny as usual, and she wanted to engage in phone sex. About ten minutes into it I asked her which one of the two dildos she was using and she said she was using both of them - the smallest in her ass and the largest in her pussy. On impulse I asked her if she ever thought about having a real one the size of her largest and she laughed and then said:

"All the time lover, all the time."

I was surprised at her answer because she had never before said anything like that.

"If you had your choice of dick size in a real one, which one would you take?"

There was no answer for several moments and I could hear Connie's heavy breathing and then she had an orgasm and shouted out:

"The big one lover, oh god, the big one." It was another minute before she could talk again, "That was a good one baby, thank you. It should hold me until you get home."

It was my turn to be silent for a moment and then I said, "Okay, I'll get you one."

Connie said, "You'll get me one what?"

"A big cock " I said, "Gotta go. Lunch times over. I'll see you when I get home" and I hung up.

When I got home that night Connie was waiting for me in bed and she was working her largest toy in and out of her pussy. She smiled at me when I came into the room,

"Just heating it up for you."

She kept working on herself as I undressed and when I got in bed she started to take the dildo out of her pussy, but I stopped her and took hold of the fake cock and started using it on her. In only minutes she was moaning and her hips were driving up at the hard rubber cock and I said

"So you want a real one, do you?"

"Oh god yes" she moaned, "Don't stop baby, don't stop. Faster honey, fuck me faster."

"Whose cock do you want?"

Connie was right on the edge of her orgasm and she screamed, "Anybody's baby, anybody's as long as it's big" and her body shook and shuddered as she came.

I climbed on and we made love for another fifteen minutes or so before I shot my rocks off and as we lay there in the warm relaxed atmosphere of successful lovemaking I said:

"I'm going to do it."

"Do what?" she asked.

"For your birthday I'm going to give you a real cock that is as big as your largest toy."

Connie rolled up onto her elbow and looked at me, "What are you talking about?"

I explained to her how her reactions to her biggest toy had convinced me that, at least for once in her life, she needed to experience the real thing. For several moments she looked at me as if I was a mad man and then she said:

"Baby, the things I say in the heat of passion don't mean I really want to do something like that."

I smiled at her, "I know, but it is something that I want to do for you."

It would take another ten pages to go through all the conversations that we had on the subject, but the end result was that she reluctantly agreed to it. The plan was for her "date" to pick her up on her birthday, take her out for a romantic evening and then let nature take its course. I would spend the night at a local motel and then come home the next afternoon. I would not tell her who her date was going to be, even though she kept asking, because I wanted it to be a surprise, and also because I thought if she knew it was someone she knew well she might back out.

The day of her birthday came and I watched as Carrie dressed for her date. She started with black lacy see-through bra and panties, garterbelt, nylons and high heels. Over this she pulled a simple black cocktail dress which she accented with a strand of pearls and as she pirouetted in front of the mirror I told her that she had never looked sexier.

"Baby, please fuck me now" she asked, "Maybe it will help me relax."

I told her that I couldn't, that she belonged to someone else this night. I kissed her and left for my motel.

Sitting in the motel bar nursing a drink I began to question what I had just done. Everything that I hadn't thought of before occurred to me now and in less than an hour I had convinced myself that I should go home and be there in case things went wrong. What if Connie decided at the last minute that she didn't want to go through with it? What if Darren refused to take no for an answer and tried to force her. What if she resisted and he hit her? I finished my drink and headed home.

I was sitting in the front room looking out the window when they pulled up in the drive. I went upstairs and got into the bedroom closet and settled down to wait. They came in the house and headed straight for the bedroom where Connie pushed Darren down on the bed. She began to do a slow strip for him and I could see the hunger on his face as her garments came off one by one until she stood before him in only her heels and hose. Connie told Darren to stand up and then she began to undress him and I began to feel stupid standing there in the closet. Obviously all my worries had been for naught, but there wasn't any way that I could leave at this point. I was stuck in the closet and I would have to watch.

When Darren's cock sprang free of its confines I knew that Connie was going to enjoy the hell out of it. It was half again bigger than her largest dildo and as I watched she went to her knees in front of Darren and took him in her mouth. I was surprised to notice that my own dick was rock hard (I had not expected that) and then Darren said something that caused my cock to wilt, "God baby, I never get tired of having your mouth on my cock" and Connie took her mouth off him long enough to say, "And I have never gotten tired of having it in my mouth."

I watched in stunned silence for the next thirty minutes as my wife sucked and fucked her big cocked lover, and even though it was highly erotic my dick stayed soft. How long, I wondered, had these two been putting the horns of a cuckold on my head? I watched as Connie had orgasm after orgasm; as she went wild, wilder than she ever had with her big dildo until Darren finally spent his seed in her. As they relaxed next to each other Darren said:

"I've been asking you this question for sixteen years now and you have never given me an answer. Maybe now, in your own home and bed, you can give me an answer. Why didn't you marry me when I asked you?"

Connie reached down and began to play with his cock, "Because I didn't love you then and I don't love you now. I like you, and I absolutely adore your cock, but not enough to have married you for it. I love my husband and if I could find someway to graft your cock onto his body that's what I would do."

On my hearing her say that my dick sprang to life and I could not believe the relief I felt at hearing her say that she was mine. Darren was silent for a moment and then he said:

"Do you think he knows that we have been getting together two or three times a week for the last sixteen years and this is just his way of saying that it's all right with him?"

It was Connie's turn to be silent. Darren's cock was getting stiff again and then she said, "Why don't you just shut up and fuck me."

I spent four hours in that closet watching my cock hungry wife try to fuck Darren's brains out. She was insatiable and in spite of all the mixed emotions that were taking place inside of me I was rock hard watching her with that huge cock. Finally it was over and Darren was getting ready to leave. He turned to Connie, who was lying on the bed, legs spread wide and with cum leaking out of her pussy.

"He's going to ask you about the evening. What are you going to say?"

Connie said, "I'm going to tell him that I loved it and that I would like to do it again. With any luck he will say yes and we won't have to sneak around anymore."

Darren nodded and said, "I'll call you" and he left. I'd had four hours to think about the situation and the bottom line was that I had wanted her to experience a big cock, so much in fact, that I had set it up so she could have one. She loved me and during our marriage I had damn sure not been short-changed in the sex department so what else mattered. I still had her and that was all I needed to know. When I heard the front door close I stepped out of the closet and saw the surprise on Connie's face. I smiled at her and said:

"Who am I to break up a sixteen year friendship. Just don't ever let him know that I know. I might want to watch again sometime."

I started taking off my clothes and I said, "Have you got enough left for me?" She smiled at me, "Always my love, always. And baby, thank you for being mine."

The End

Here is a sample from another story you may enjoy:

Erotic Affairs

Just Plain Bob

Creamed

Erotica Short Stories, **Vol. 24**

The wife and I were attending a pool party at her boss's house. I don't even know why I had agreed to come to it with her because I didn't like the asshole. He was one of those back-slapping good time Charlies who would grab your hand, give it a manly shake and say, "God guy, but it's good to see you again" and all the time you knew that he didn't even remember your name. But the wife liked her job and the pay was decent. The only drawback to the job was that the office was just a touch "political" and her not being at the party would be noticed and commented on. She didn't want to go alone so she hacked away at me until I gave up the fight and agreed to go.

Despite not wanting to be there I wasn't having too bad a time. I mean just how bad can it be sitting around a pool with a cool drink on a sunny day and watching bikini clad women? Plus I was drinking the asshole's booze and I made sure that it wasn't the cheap stuff. About three hours into the party it dawned on me that even with the bucketful of sunscreen rubbed on me I'd still had a tad too much sun. I'd come to the party in a short sleeved shirt, but I remembered that I had a long sleeved shirt in the trunk of the car. Not wanting to track through the house with wet feet I headed around the side of the house. I saw a couple of kids looking in a window and when the saw me they bent over and picked up a soccer ball that was lying on the ground and took off.

I went out to the car and got the shirt and then headed back to the pool. Curiosity grabbed me when I came to the window that the kids had been looking in and I stopped to take a look. The blinds were closed, but I noticed a gap at the bottom where they hadn't gone all the way down and I bent over and peered through the gap. The room was a den or a home office. There was a desk against one wall with a phone and a computer on it. Two bookcases against another wall, but the focal point was the long leather couch against the east wall. There were three guys sitting on the couch, all relatives of my wife's boss. His oldest son was sitting in the center, his nineteen-year-old was sitting to the left of his older brother and on the right sat his nephew. There was a woman on her knees in front of the guy in the center and she was bent forward sucking his cock while her hands fondled the cocks of the two guys on either side of him.

The woman was my wife.

If you enjoyed this sample then look for **Creamed**.

Also by this Author:

The Prodigal Family: The Abbotts

Watching My Shared Wife

The Waitress and the Runaway Husband

Baiting Mr. Little

Too Hot for Henry

Chuck's Fantasy

The Redhead's Desires

Rescued at Riley's

His Every Fantasy

Open Mike Night

Pursuit for Revenge

Why Does He Do That?

Halloween & Drugs

Tracey

When Rob Met Kari

Becoming a Shared Wife, Vol. 1 –

(Wife Sharing and Other Adventures)

Becoming a Shared Wife, Vol. 2 –

(Hazardous Wives)

Becoming a Shared Wife, Vol. 3 –

(Wives Who Stray)

From the Author

WANT FREE COPIES OF MY BOOKS?

Just visit my blog and download free copies of my books:

awesomeauthors.org/justplainbob

Yes, I write about sluts and whores because as everyone knows, you tend to write about the things you know. And I do like sluts and whores, just not the ones that lie to me and cheat on me.

So be forewarned - if you click on a Just Plain Bob story you will be getting sluts, whores and husbands who do not kill, maim and destroy. There are other things you will rarely find in a Just Plain Bob story.

If you enjoyed any of my books then please share the love and promote my books in Amazon. I would really appreciate your honest reviews, too!

Good news is always welcome.

One Last Thing, For Kindle Readers...

When you turn the page, Kindle will give you the opportunity to rate this book and share your thoughts on Facebook and Twitter. If you enjoyed my writings, would you please take a few seconds to let your friends know about it? Because... when they enjoy they will be grateful to you and so will I.

Thank you!

Just Plain Bob
justplainbob@awesomeauthors.org

You may also like the books by these authors:

ABBY

CITY GIRL IN THE COUNTRY

EROTIC ROMANCE

KERRY JAMES

Abby had little difficulty in getting to this point, on the B3227 from Taunton heading towards South Molton, and guessed that somewhere on this road she should see a sign indicating her turn. Yet as she drove further and further into Devon she became uneasy that no such sign had revealed itself. Navigation became more of a problem as she drove deeper into the countryside, signposts, when you could find them; indicated a destination which then received no further mention at all upon succeeding signs. High banks on either side of the road meant that she had little clue as to where she was, the only point of reference was the ribbon of road unwinding ceaselessly and vanishing under the bonnet of her car and the occasional signs for some oddly named village or hamlet. As she passed through villages such as Wiveliscombe and Bampton, she wondered if she had gone wrong, and seeing the sign that said South Molton was just five miles farther on, decided that indeed she had gone wrong. Swearing mildly under her breath, Abby was giving thought to turning round and retracing her path.

Suddenly, she caught that breath; there was the sign. Leaning gently against the high banks that enclosed the road with a vigorous growth of Ivy as camouflage, she would have missed it had she not been driving slowly looking for a place to turn. It was a peculiar sensation, and her heart was beating furiously as she made the turn. A name that had previously existed only in hearsay and on a map was now a fact. Her mother had mentioned the name a few times without thinking, but would not be pressed on its significance. When her mother had died, Abby was nineteen, there was no reference at all to the name in her personal effects, which were few, there was no birth certificate, and the only official document she could find was an out of date passport, giving the birth area as South Molton. Abby's history consisted of just her mother's death certificates, and her own birth certificate. Abby now realised that she could have obtained a copy of her mother's birth certificate, but as is the way of things she had not thought logically at the time. She would repair this oversight as soon as possible. She wondered why her mum had a passport, as she had never travelled abroad.

Combe Linney, as Abby spelt it, was not even marked on her road map, and she had to resort to the Ordinance Survey to discover the location; again there was no place spelt Linney, but there was a Combe Lyney, near South Molton, and she assumed that this had to be the place. Its sum total consisted of two black oblongs, and a round dot with a cross on top, presumably indicating a church. There were no A or B roads that ventured anywhere near the place. If this wasn't the back of beyond, then it was pretty close to it.

The mystery could not be investigated immediately as Abby had after her mother's death, to consider the business of life, a job, somewhere to live. Her mother had left her little, but a stubborn trait that helped Abby survive the numerous jobs she took in the financial and insurance trade; making tea and coffee for surly men and women who viewed her simply as the office gofer.; They would have been surprised if they had known that Abby did not merely put their drinks in front of them, but closely studied what they were doing. They didn't know because Abby was invisible, unimportant, not even missed when she left to go to a better job, using all she had learned to pack her C.V. She was twenty-five when she started in the city as a proprietary equity trader, the years of watching and learning placed her in good stead. She would not say that she was a brilliant trader, there were many more that could turn sixpences into sovereigns at the drop of a hat, but she was intuitive, and with no family to call upon her time, was content to work all hours to achieve her goal. In a business where employers counted the hours almost as important as the success, she was regarded highly.

If you enjoyed this sample then look for <u>Abby</u>.

THREESOMES EROTICA

AND MARIA
MAKES THREE

Joan Vegas

Dear Ms. Joan:

This is the report you asked me to write up about me, my husband and our very dear friend (and special family member), Maria.

Let me begin by telling you about each of us.

About me (Annette)... Since the first time I had intercourse in the backseat of a boyfriend's car, I have always enjoyed the feelings of pleasure that sex has given me. While I had feelings of conflict over the non-marital sex those first few times, I still enjoyed the feel of a man's organ probing around inside me. Then I learned to give my dates manual and oral pleasure. I found that I liked that too.

A few years later one of the guys I dated treated me to "head." I was hesitant at first to let him do that, but he insisted. The intense pleasure of that experience left me wanting "head" as often as a date would give it to me.

That was my sexual background prior to meeting Jordan (or Jordy, as I call him). From our earliest dates, we made sex a regular part of our dates. Six months after we met, we married. At the time, Jordy was 24 and I was 23.

Oh yes, the obligatory physical description. I stand 5' 6" tall, generally weigh about 130 lbs., and have rather full C-cup boobs. My eyes are blue, and my hair is a sort of dishwater blond. I generally keep my hair curled and styled. While I have always thought of myself as sort of average, Jordy is constantly telling me that I am "really good lookin' with beautiful legs and tits." Who am I to disagree with him?

Both Jordy and I are college grads with post-grad degrees. For the past several years I have been doing contract engineering work out of our home. My field of engineering allows me to get work rather easily, and choose between part time or full time work.

About Jordy... Jordy is very handsome (in my subjective opinion, but Maria says so too). He stands 5' 9" tall, typically weighs about 170 lbs., and has brown hair and brown eyes. He has a ruddy complexion, a mustache and a full beard. Jordy sports a cock that when stimulated measures 8" long and 5" around. Unlike most other men I have seen, his dick tapers from a relatively small head to its thick girth (gives wonderful sensations as it enters and slides within my pussy!).

Both Jordy and I generally work full time. He works for a computer firm that sells and services software for specialty retailing businesses. His work often takes him out on the road (up to 1,000 miles away). We are both typical Anglo-Saxon Caucasians.

About Maria... Maria is a beautiful young woman (four years younger than me). Her father was half black and half American Indian. Her mother was mostly Spanish (her mother from Mexico and father from Brazil).

The result of their union was a sexy gal who has soft skin that boasts the appearance of a year-round deep Coppertone tan. Jordy says her skin looks (and tastes like) golden honey.

She has small cone-shaped breasts with large (very sensitive) nipples. Her legs are at least as long as mine, yet she just stands just 5'3" tall. Jordy describes her as "a compact gal whose legs go all the way to 'heaven'". The little nymph typically weighs in at a scant 105 lbs.

Maria was born in Porto Rico, and grew up in New Jersey. Her father died when she was very young. Her mother struggled to raise her and her two older sisters. When they grew up, the sisters left home, and really have not made much of themselves. Maria saw that, and determined that she was going to get some higher education and make something of herself.

They both also had very unsatisfying marriages to husbands who were abusive. Maria's mother got sick when Maria was just 17, and Maria decided to stay living at home and help her mother.

Meanwhile, Maria enrolled at a local community college while staying at home to care for her mother.

Her mother died just after Maria turned 20. With nothing holding her back any more, and no desire to hook up with some guy just to get married, Maria decided to travel west to begin a new life. Her savings took her only to Oklahoma City where she got work in a restaurant. After several months, she decided she didn't like Oklahoma City. She had accumulated enough money for a bus ticket to Santa Fe, New Mexico, where we happened to be living at the time.

Again, Maria took work waiting tables in a restaurant. That's where we met her, three weeks after her arrival. While dining at the restaurant where she was working, we got to talking with her. We found her to be quite attractive, pleasantly personable, and quite intelligent. She agreed to meet us for a drink after her shift ended.

We walked down the street to a nearby lounge where we each had a few drinks and got to know each other. We learned that Maria had her 21st birthday the week before, so we asked her if she would like to celebrate by joining us for a late night dip at a nearby hot springs. She said she did not have her swimsuit with her. I let her know that the place has several pools, some of which were "clothing optional," and that we seldom wore swim suits there. After giggling a bit about that prospect, she agreed, and we all piled into our car for the short trip.

I should tell you that Maria has long, straight, shiny black hair that hangs about 5" below her shoulders. Her eyes are also pools of deep black. In spite of her father's racial background, Maria's face and hair give no indication of her Black heritage. Only her skin evidences her mixed heritage... and does so in a highly attractive way.

As she and I stripped in the dressing room, I noticed she had a full, untrimmed bush covering her crotch. We both used our towels to cover ourselves on the short walk to the pool that Jordy had picked out. We slipped in on either side of him, and began to chat like we had been long-time friends. During our time in the pool, a few others joined us for a while. When I sat on the edge of the pool to cool off, Maria joined me with no evidence of concern about her nudity in the dim light.

During our conversations we let Maria know that we had a sort of open marriage, and had each occasionally enjoyed having others as sex partners. She just took it all in without any particular reaction.

Getting to Know Maria... At the end of the evening we took Maria to her apartment and made arrangements for the three of us to go out together again the following Saturday night. That night Jordy and I made passionate love as I told him that no other woman had ever turned me on before... but that Maria had. He suggested that just maybe, Maria might be a woman we could both enjoy... while giving her pleasure.

If you enjoyed this sample then look for **And Maria Makes Three**.

The
Daring
DOPPELGANGERS
Hot Taboo Erotica

Jack Ryder

I saw her as I was pulling into the Pendleton truck stop. Even though it was unseasonably warm, it was still out of the ordinary for anyone to be wearing such short cutoff jeans. As my eyes travelled up the rest of her body, it was easy to see that she was a knock out. My jaw dropped when I finally studied her face. This girl could be an identical clone of that Claudia Black who was on that hit TV show Farscape.

Even with the dark aviator sun glasses she was wearing, I could swear they looked identical.

I tried not to stare at her when I passed her going in the door to buy some coffee and use the restroom.

I could not see her eyes through the dark sunglasses, but she seemed to have a whimsical smirk on her face as I went past her. I made it a point to keep my eyes on her face but I could still feel a wiggle down between my legs as I caught a whiff of her honeysuckle scented perfume. I was disappointed to find that she had left the sales area when I came back out to get my coffee and a snack cake.

She was standing by the curb as I was pulling out of the parking area. I saw two cars stop almost instantly but she waved them away just before I reached the exit driveway. I almost bit my tongue when I pulled up in front of her to see if she would accept a ride. I figured that was why she had her thumb out. Her black leather biker style jacket was completely unzipped in front and I could see most of both her big firm breasts.

When I pressed the button to lower the passenger window, she bent forward to peer in at me.

"Where do you need to go?" I asked her. I could not keep myself from glancing at her bare chest. "My breasts need to get as far away from here as possible," she taunted me when I glanced up into her eyes. "The rest of me would like to go along as well."

If you enjoyed this sample then look for **The Daring Doppelgangers**.

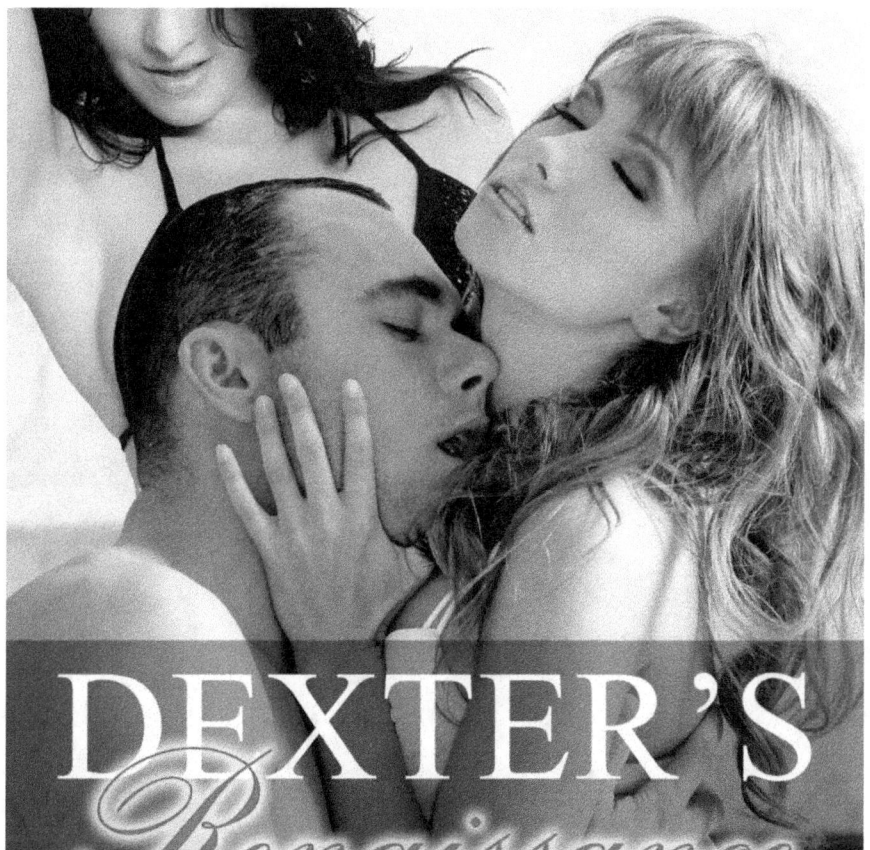

DEXTER'S
Renaissance

LEE NORTH

Hot Romance Erotica

That May picnic was the beginning of a series of dates that Michelle and I enjoyed. Sometimes to a movie or play, often for dinner, occasionally for a ballgame. It was on one of those dates that there was a distinct shift in our relationship. Until then, we had held hands, kissed lightly, and generally behaved ourselves. I think we both could feel the pressure building. It changed after we had spent a pleasant evening at a local play.

We were in her late model Lincoln and I was driving. In the past, I would stop at the Rossmoor and she would drive on to her apartment. That night she had other ideas.

"Drive to my place, Dex. It's Friday, and we've got all weekend. You haven't been to my place yet and I'd like to spend some time with you," she said, placing her hand over mine.

It didn't take me any time at all to agree and head toward Lakeshore Drive. As we neared the building, Michelle took a small transmitter from her purse and pushed a button. The open grilled gate began to rise and I drove into the underground parking area as she directed me to her numbered space. The transmitter also unlocked the door to the elevator and stairs. After waiting a moment for an available car, a door slid open and we entered with Michelle inserting a card and pushing a button marked "R."

When we stepped out of the car, a large glass window was directly in front of us and I could see we were at the top of the building. To the left was 2102 and to the right, 2101. Michelle guided me right and opened the door, stepping in and turning on some lights.

It was a very nice and apparently large penthouse suite, one of two on the top floor of the building. As I looked around I saw the trappings of affluence; fine furniture, interesting artwork, and lush carpeting.

Michelle kicked off her shoes and I followed suit.

"Dex, I'm all sticky from the humidity today. I'm going to have a shower and change. Why don't you do the same, then we can relax and get to know each other better," she smiled.

I wasn't about to decline the offer and happily agreed. She led me to the main bathroom, handed me some towels and a washcloth and told me how to work the controls on the shower system. I needed the lesson. It was a multi-head system with pre-selected temperatures. The cabinet itself was almost as big as the bathroom in my apartment.

As I soaped and rinsed, I almost expected that Michelle would suddenly appear and join me, but that didn't happen. I stepped out of the shower, towelled myself off, and dressed in my slacks and shirt. I didn't bother with socks. They wouldn't be as fresh as I was so I stuffed them in my back pocket as I headed barefoot for the living area.

Waiting for Michelle, I wandered about the spacious penthouse. There was a dining area with a very nice buffet and china cabinet, along with a large period-style table and chairs. The kitchen was through a wide passage and it too was large, with a big island and plenty of cabinet and counter space. Most houses didn't have this much room.

I was just coming out of my inspection of the kitchen when Michelle reappeared and got my undivided attention. She was wearing a black silk pyjama suit, if that's what it's called. It was floor length, very sleek with material flowing from its wide legs and arms. She had a smile for me as she approached, then stopped and swirled in a circle to emphasize the graceful lines of her attire.

"You like?" she asked, already knowing my answer.

"Very nice … very elegant." I almost added very sexy. As she had moved to show off the garment it was immediately apparent that she was wearing nothing beneath it. Her nipples protruded clearly in front and her buttocks were perfectly outlined in back. I could feel my erection beginning to develop.

"Would you care for coffee … or perhaps a glass of wine or brandy?" she asked in a tempting tone.

"I'd like a glass of brandy, please."

"Oh, good. I'll have one too," she said, turning to move into the kitchen.

I followed her as if she was drawing me along. Perhaps it was the magnetic appeal of her, dressed as she was in such alluring garb. She reached up in a cupboard for the brandy bottle and I stepped behind her to help her. I was directly behind her now, touching her slightly with my hips and chest. On the spur of the moment, I did something I would never have thought I would do.

With the fingertips of my right hand, I lightly, slowly, ran them up her side, feeling her ribs as I went. Then, in a moment of complete recklessness, I moved my hand and gently cupped and stroked a fulsome breast. I felt her shiver from the contact but she didn't push me away or resist my touch. In fact, I was sure I heard a soft moan.

I couldn't see her face, but she had begun to lean back into me, the brandy bottle now forgotten. Her hands were on the countertop as if bracing her against an assault. My left hand joined the right in teasing her nipples and now her groan was more audible. Emboldened, I allowed my left hand to slip down over her abdomen and softly rub the silky smooth material of her gown.

I felt her backside push slowly back into me and she could certainly now feel my erection. I moved my hips to place my hardened member between her cheeks. She welcomed that with a swaying motion that only reinforced my hardness. One of us was going to have to do something soon.

It was Michelle who took my right hand and guided it inside her top, giving me access to her breasts. She pulled at the fold of the material and I felt a little pop as a small snap released the upper half of the garment. Still holding my hand, she slid it down to her waist where another small snap gave way and the gown parted completely.

I felt her shrug her shoulders and the lovely black item fell at her feet. She was naked before me, still facing away but leaning back more urgently against me, pressing herself into my prominent manhood. Once more, I did something I would not have thought I could attempt. I intimated with my knee that I wanted her to spread her legs and she immediately complied. She understood exactly what I was intending.

I unbuttoned my pants and they too fell at my feet, my briefs following them almost immediately. I took my cock in my hand and began to stroke her already wet centre in preparation for my entry. Again, she did everything she could to help me and within a few moments I was pushing into her. Slowly and carefully at first, but her insistence gave me courage to thrust a little more and soon I was buried well inside her.

I moved a little more forcefully and quickly as she continued to encourage me. There was absolutely no doubt in my mind that this was what she had planned all along. Her voice soon joined the action, not so much with words but with little cries of encouragement and pleasure. How long it had been since she had been with a man I did not know. I only knew she was with me now, and I was reaping the reward of her pent up need.

I leaned my head forward and captured an earlobe between my lips, then licked the back of her neck as I continued to stroke into her. In response, she threw her head back, growling a pagan, earthy moan of lust, slamming her ass back into me, the smacking sound of our joining now growing louder. This was probably going to end quite soon, but I did whatever I could to hold off as long as possible.

A few moments later her moves became more erratic and we almost fell out of rhythm as she began her orgasmic journey. I stayed with her as long as I could, but I was going to finish as well and there was nothing I could do to prevent it. I felt myself release into her once, twice, then a third time. As I did, she sagged against me and I wrapped my arms around her waist so that she didn't collapse against the granite counter or on the floor.

In all my experience, limited as it might have been, I had never had a more erotic, spontaneous coupling than this. I was in no condition to continue. Michelle was leaning back into me, breathing heavily and holding my arms tightly as they encircled her. Not a word had passed between us from the time she walked to the liquor cupboard.

I'm still not sure what got into me that night. I was either very confident of myself or very reckless. Probably the latter. Nonetheless, I picked the naked beauty up in my arms and carefully steered my way out of the kitchen toward the master bedroom. When I arrived, I saw that the bed had been turned down and I carefully laid Michelle on it crosswise with her legs dangling over the side. Her eyes were open and she was staring at me, no doubt wondering what I was doing. Still, neither of us had yet spoken.

I pulled off my shirt and now as naked as she, I got on my knees on the lushly carpeted floor, my hands gently but insistently pushing her legs apart. Again, she offered no resistance. I moved between her thighs and began to kiss the flawless, smooth skin. I was about to work my way up to the place where I had just planted my seed when I felt her hands in my hair. Was this a 'stop' or a 'go?'

I could see a bit of my semen on the lips of her vagina and I wondered what possessed me to try this. What was I trying to prove? Yet, even with that question in my head, I continued. As Michelle realized what I was planning, she must have had second thoughts. That had prompted her to place her hands on my head again, trying to decide if she should put a stop to my intentions. As I made up my mind to continue, I felt her resistance lessen.

I moved toward my target and slowly, with the flat of my tongue, I began to make love to her once again. This was going to be a very different kind of penetration. I had plenty of experience with oral sex but none just after I had planted my seed inside a woman. It was too late to stop now, and Michelle was making no sign that she wanted me to.

In fact, I was bringing her back to life with my tongue and fingers. Her hips were rising and falling erratically, responding to whatever stimuli she felt. Her grip on my head tightened and I could feel her fingers in my hair. She was holding on tight, her body dancing to whatever music my tongue created. I flicked the tip of her clitoris and got the response I expected. Her hips snapped up in reaction.

I was beginning to tire ... or at least my tongue was. Michelle was nearing another orgasm and I willed myself to continue. At last she let go and I could stop and rest. I crawled up beside her, lying on my back. She rolled over me and gave me a deep, soulful kiss. Whatever I had accomplished, she approved of it. I wondered if it was something her late husband had not provided.

We lay there for a while, her head on my shoulder, our legs dangling over the edge of the bed. I kissed her forehead and ran my fingers through her soft, flowing hair. Her hand was holding my now flaccid cock, not manipulating it, just holding it lightly.

"That was wonderful," she said at last. "I didn't realize just how much I wanted you and you were perfect for me."

"We took some chances tonight," I said. "That gown didn't leave much to the imagination."

"It was either that or I would just come out naked. It was a coin toss."

"Were you worried I wouldn't get the message?"

"That thought did cross my mind. I can never be sure just what you are thinking about when it comes to women, Dex. Sometimes shy, but tonight a completely different person. You took command and I was the lucky one when you did."

"You were irresistible. I'm sure that was your plan, wasn't it? Well, it worked. I couldn't resist you, so everything that happened was a result of that."

"You'll stay tonight, won't you?"

"Yes. You might regret it in the morning, but I do want to stay. I want to wake up with you."

"We've started something, haven't we?" It was as much a statement as a question.

"I hope so. Is that what you want?" I wondered.

"Yes. As little as I know about you, as little time as I've known you, everything I've learned tells me that you are right for me."

"Well, we're going to have some time to find out so let's enjoy ourselves and see where it goes. I'm not a one-night-stand kind of guy. I'm looking for something more than that."

"You wouldn't be in this apartment tonight if I thought otherwise. But now that you're here, I'm going to keep you here as long as I can."

After a few minutes, Michelle rose and padded to the ensuite bathroom, closing the door behind her. She returned a minute or so later and crawled on top of me, rubbing my still limp cock with her lightly haired sex. I began to respond to her tantalizing little game and she noticed.

"Oh ... isn't that nice. Can I have some more please, sir?"

"Of course you may. Just tell me your heart's desire, young lady, and I'll try and fulfill your wishes."

"Well, after that glorious fucking you gave me in the kitchen, I think I'd like you to make love to me. Something nice and slow and lasting."

"How would you like me to start? A little foreplay, perhaps?"

"I think I've had all the foreplay I can handle tonight, Dex. I'm still carrying some of you around in me and what I really want is to have you inside me again."

If you enjoyed this sample then look for **Dexter's Renaissance**.

Saving *Heather*

HOT ROMANCE EROTICA
LILITH JONES

She went into his arms. Her kiss had been intended to be a light acceptance of his niceness. He kept it up, though, and she certainly had no reason to end it. He sucked her lower lip, and then he licked her lips. She opened them to him, but he kept licking them. She finally sought his tongue with hers. When they met, sparks flew. He pulled her to him, and she felt his firmness against her stomach.

"Oh, my love," he said when they broke. His hands went to the buttons on her blouse. She was his, and she let him strip her. He did it slowly, kissing every newly revealed inch of skin. She felt aroused, more aroused than she had been in years. She also felt cherished, cherished as not even the Rick of years ago had cherished her.

When he was kneeling and he had her jeans down around her ankles, he eased back to let her step out of them. Then he kissed her legs upward to her panties. He kissed her mound through those panties, and she felt ready for him. He eased her down on the bed.

If he'd been patience personified in removing her clothes, he was nearly a blur in removing his. Then he faced her, fully nude and magnificently male. He looked as ready for her as she felt ready for him. She pushed the panties down, and Rick took them off her feet. She spread her legs slightly as he got into bed.

He started with a kiss, though. It was a gentle, but extremely sensual, kiss. She arched her hips off the bed as their tongues met. He cupped her, holding all her femininity. As he moved his mouth from hers to her breasts, her nipple strained upward towards his mouth. He licked it, touching only the tip with the tip of his tongue. She quivered all over, and he moved to the other breast. When he sucked that nipple, sparks shot from the tips of her toes.

He thrust one finger deep inside her. Then he drew it out, very slowly, and over her clit. It was only one finger, but it went so slowly that it felt much more -- maybe a yard long. He changed breasts again and sucked deeply. The sucking and the stroking were sending heat through her. She felt as though she was being baked, and there was a fire in her womb.

He raised his head from her breast and stared into her eyes. "Heather," he said. "Heather, my love."

Then lightning crackled within her. She moaned and writhed. It went on as he kept stroking. She collapsed, and he removed his finger. He kissed her forehead and her shoulder. As her breath eased, he kissed her nose tip, and then her breasts, and then her stomach.

He again stroked her mound. He rubbed the lips there against one another, very softly. The response, however, was fire. His hand was wonderful, and his look was loving if it was searching. He had brought her delight, and she could believe he would bring her more delight. She wanted more than that, though.

"You," she said. "Please!" He rolled away suddenly. She stifled a protest when she saw that he was reaching in his drawer. She almost told him that he didn't need the rubber. She could tell, though, that this was one more act of caring. He was taking responsibility, taking care of her. Whatever the physical shortcomings, she would celebrate it as an action of the man who would never put her at risk.

Now, he was kneeling between her legs. She spread her lips with her hand and rolled her hips to receive him fully. She felt open to him.

"Heather," he said.

"Yes, oh yes."

However open she had been, she felt him stretch her more as he went in slowly. And it was slow, agonizingly slow. When he had filled her, he kissed her briefly. She hugged him with her arms and with her legs. He was in her, but she wanted to hold all of him.

He withdrew as slowly, and he felt a need for him to return. He thrust in a little faster, and she felt herself burn. As he sped up, it was never fast enough. She thrust up to engulf him as he came down. Then the lightning crashed through her again.

He withdrew half way, rammed into her, and pulsed deep within her. For a second, he was one rigid arch within her hug. Then he collapsed onto his elbows. She, too, relaxed. Her feet rested on his calves, and her hands rested on his back, but she was no longer really hugging him.

That was closeness. They were one. She was disappointed when he moved away, although the freedom to breathe was a relief. He moved off the bed and turned off the overhead light. As he came back, she heard the rubber drop into the wastebasket.

"We really need another pillow," he said as he got into bed. He lay down beside her and pulled her into a hug. He carefully spread the sheet over both of them.

"We don't really need a wider bed, though," she said. He chuckled. "Y'know . . . Maybe you don't know. I'm on the pill."

"Well, it didn't seem a good time to ask."

"It wasn't. You took care of me."

"I always will," he said. "Somebody should. You work too hard taking care of Anne. Somebody has to take care of you."

"Well, maybe, we'll take care of each other."

"That's a good idea. I love you. Seriously, if we're going to be a family, we'll have to divide up the family tasks. Probably, you should do the dividing. But give me some of the tasks of caring for Anne. Just because I don't know how, doesn't mean I can't learn."

"You do great. I might have to give her the baths and wash her clothes, but you give her kisses and protect her."

"Washing her clothes and yours can't be all that different from washing mine, and I wash mine already. Anyway, first you get the divorce, preferably with full custody. Next we get married. Then, if I can, I adopt her. After that, we'll try to get her to call me Daddy."

"I love you." Heather thought Rick's project to get Anne to call him Daddy reflected more of the story that she'd heard at the funeral than Anne's situation. Right now, Anne had two men in her life. One beat her, and she called him Daddy. The other hugged her, and she called him Rick. Anne would know which name meant love. Well, courts took forever, and four-year-olds were resilient. By the time Rick had gone through his agenda, Anne would call him anything he wanted.

"And I love you, too," Rick said. She believed him. His hand stroked up to her breast, and she patted it and held it there. "Is this what married people do?" he asked. "I mean lie in bed and talk later?"

"Well, I'm not sure that I want my last marriage to be a model." And that was an understatement. Too many of her conversations with Bill had been at the top of their lungs. "Is this what you want our marriage to be?"

"Yeah. Especially this part." He squeezed her breast very lightly. "I like holding you."

"And," she said in satisfaction, "I like being held by you."

If you enjoyed this sample then look for **Saving Heather**.

WANT FREE COPIES OF MY BOOKS?
Just visit my blog and download free copies of my books:
awesomeauthors.org/justplainbob